*From Now On,
When You Look at Me
You're Going to See Me.*

You're going to be aware of me with every cell in your body.''

His warm breath caressed her skin as he whispered the slightly threatening words, and Mara's eyes opened wide with alarm. Grant caught the betraying reaction and smiled. "I'm going to crawl right inside your skin, lady. I'm going to become as necessary to you as breathing. Before I'm through, you're going to beg me to make love to you.''

His voice was low and intimate, the silky tones adding a chilling degree of menace to the incredible statement.

GINNA GRAY

admits that for most of her life she has been both an avid reader and a dreamer. For a long time the desire to write, to put her fantasies down on paper, had been growing, until finally she told herself to *do* it. Now, she can't imagine not writing.

Dear Reader:

I'd like to take this opportunity to thank you for all your support and encouragement of Silhouette Romances.

Many of you write in regularly, telling us what you like best about Silhouette, which authors are your favorites. This is a tremendous help to us as we strive to publish the best contemporary romances possible.

All the romances from Silhouette Books are for you, so enjoy this book and the many stories to come.

Karen Solem
Editor-in-Chief
Silhouette Books

GINNA GRAY
Images

Silhouette Romance

Published by Silhouette Books New York

America's Publisher of Contemporary Romance

Silhouette Books by Ginna Gray

SILHOUETTE BOOKS
300 E. 42nd St., New York, N.Y. 10017

Copyright © 1985 by Virginia Gray
Cover artwork copyright © 1985 by Artist International, Inc.

Distributed by Pocket Books

ISBN: 0-373-08352-1

First Silhouette Books printing April, 1985

10 9 8 7 6 5 4 3 2 1

Map by Ray Lundgren

America's Publisher of Contemporary Romance

Printed in the U.S.A.

BC91

To Roger, Ayako, Leslie,
Roy, Dennis, Hideko and Steven—
for all your support and love

Images

Chapter One

For just an instant Mara was glad to be home. Then, coming to a halt one step inside the door, she let her eyes wander slowly over the elegant entryway, and a shiver trickled its way down her spine as the familiar black desolation settled over her.

It didn't help telling herself that she was being fanciful, that she was allowing fatigue and the lateness of the hour to influence her mood. Mara knew it wasn't true. For the past two years her reaction had been the same every time she came back here. The house was immaculate, as always, yet it had a musty, unlived-in smell, and when it hit her she felt abruptly alone, aware of the emptiness, the silence.

Mara set her suitcases down on the polished marble floor and turned to close the door. She flipped the lock and attached the chain, then turned back with an exhausted sigh. Automatically her eyes were drawn to the stairs. Even as tired as she was, the temptation was strong to climb those steps and escape to her studio. Only there could she keep this chilling loneliness at bay. Work had become her salvation, and almost every waking moment was spent in her sanctuary before an easel. Her soft mouth twisted into a rueful grimace. "Which is exactly why the house has this unlived-in air," she muttered sadly.

Sighing, Mara hefted her cases and carried them into the bedroom at the end of the hall. She had hoped to feel differently after this trip, but the need to get away from this place and the haunting, bittersweet memories was stronger than ever. Thank goodness she had instructed the builder to start on the new house. With any luck she'd be able to move by the end of summer. Maybe out of Houston, in new, unfamiliar surroundings, she could come to terms with her grief.

It was later, as Mara stood under the warm spray of the shower, that she became aware of the warning flashes of light just behind her eyes. They were a sure sign the throbbing ache in her temples would soon become a blinding migraine. With a sense of urgency, Mara rinsed the soap from her body and stepped from the shower. The only hope she had of warding it off was to take two of those detestable tablets and go to bed. She hated to take them. The aftereffects left her groggy and out of focus. But she knew that if she didn't, the rest of the night would be spent hanging over the commode being violently ill.

Mara wrapped a towel around her body, then took the prescription bottle from the medicine cabinet and shook two of the tablets out into the palm of her hand. She wasn't really surprised by the migraine. Her first Paris showing had been a huge success, both artistically and financially, but it had also been a tremendous strain. In addition, she had spent much of her time fending off the advances of more than one amorous Frenchman. Returning the bottle to the cabinet, Mara caught sight of her reflection in the mirror and grimaced.

Much to her chagrin, the combination of creamy,

flawless skin, classic features, green eyes, and flame-red hair had always made her stand out in a crowd. Privately, Mara considered her vivid coloring and extravagant beauty to be one of nature's little practical jokes. The inner and outer woman didn't match at all. Contrary to her appearance, she was in no way an extrovert, nor did she possess the volatile disposition typical of a redhead. Mara was naturally quiet and reserved and, except when provoked in the extreme, very even-tempered. She was, quite simply, a paradox, her low-key life-style and unassuming personality a surprising contradiction to her vibrant, eye-catching exterior.

As she absently raised a hand to push the tumble of fiery hair over her shoulder, Mara recalled David's teasing words from long ago. "It looks as though it would burn your fingers to touch it," he had laughingly commented countless times.

The wisp of memory brought a haunted look to the emerald eyes, and her long, dark lashes fluttered downward. For a moment Mara just stood there, fighting back the pain, her sensuously curved mouth compressed into a tight line and her delicate auburn brows drawn together in an anguished frown.

Taking a deep breath, Mara opened her eyes and stared bleakly at her reflected image. *Oh, David. David.*

With quick, jerky movements she pulled a paper cup from the dispenser and filled it with water from the tap. The telephone rang just as she swallowed the tablets, and she jumped with fright. Mara tossed the cup into the wastebasket and quickly blotted up the spilled water with a towel, then left the bathroom and hurried barefoot across the plush, misty green carpet, her toes curling into the thick, soft pile. As she neared the bedside table and reached for the phone her eyes darted to the clock.

Chuck. It had to be him. He was the only idiot who would call at two o'clock in the morning. He had

absolutely no sense of time and was filled with boundless
energy. Chuck thought nothing of working all day and
playing half the night. It never occurred to him that others
didn't do the same.

"Hello."

"Mara? Is that you?" Chuck's voice boomed cheerily
down the line.

"No. It's your friendly neighborhood burglar."

"Don't be silly. Women aren't burglars. All that
jimmying windows is bad for the fingernails."

"Male chauvinist pig," Mara muttered in feigned
irritation.

Chuck laughed softly. "No kidding, sweetheart. I was
driving by on my way home and saw the lights. I thought
I'd better check and be sure it was you."

Mara's glance went back to the clock, and her lips
twisted wryly. "I'm surprised you could tear yourself
away. What's the matter? Can't sleep in a strange bed?
And by the way, what's her name? When I left last month
you were in the depths of despair over breaking up with
Suzie something-or-other."

Chuck laughed again. "Her name isn't Something-or-
other. It's Peterson. Susan Peterson. Anyway, that was
just an infatuation. This time I'm really in love."

Mara sat down on the edge of the bed, smiling in spite
of her throbbing head. Dear Chuck. He was just like a
happy bee, flitting from flower to flower. Every new girl
was the love of his life . . . for about a month. During
their marriage she and David had nursed him through
countless broken love affairs, and since her husband's
death, Mara had done it alone. Chuck was her oldest and
dearest friend, the brother she never had.

"You won't mind if I don't buy my dress for the
wedding just yet, will you?"

"Ouch! That one was below the belt."

"Sorry, I'm not myself. Jet lag and all that."

"Oh, say, it is late, isn't it," Chuck said apologetically, as though suddenly becoming aware of the time. "I'll let you get some sleep just as soon as you tell me how the Paris show went."

"It was great. A sellout in fact."

"That's my girl." Chuck's voice went low and warm with affection. "I told you they'd love your work. Did you have time to relax and see the sights?"

"Yes. For the last two weeks I've been touring France. You should see the marvelous sketches I made. I can hardly wait to get started on them."

Chuck groaned. "Sweetheart, you were supposed to relax and have a good time—not work," he admonished. "But while we're on the unpleasant subject, do you mind if I come over in the morning to paint?" Mara could almost hear the grin in his voice when he added wickedly, "Being in love inspires me."

Mara had met Chuck years before in art school. In her opinion, he was very talented, but Chuck claimed he was temperamentally unsuited to be a serious artist. She had to admit he seemed to have found his niche in the commercial field. As the art director for a small but very successful advertising agency, he not only earned an excellent salary but appeared to be completely satisfied with his work. The high-powered, pressured atmosphere suited his personality much more than the lonely isolation of an artist. But occasionally, when in the mood, Chuck came to her studio to do some serious painting.

"Fine, so long as you don't wake me. You do, and so help me I'll string you up by your thumbs."

"You'll never know I'm there. 'Bye, love."

At first it was only a faint, intermittent tapping. Then, slowly, as she began to surface from the sweet oblivion of a deep, mindless sleep, it increased in volume, becoming a loud, insistent banging that could not be ignored. With a groan, Mara flipped over onto her stomach and burrowed her head beneath the pillow. The thick layer of down muffled the sound but didn't shut it out completely. Irritation puckered Mara's brow as her foggy brain struggled to identify the noise. When it finally hit her, she groaned in agony. Someone was knocking at the door, and each rap went through her head with the force of a sledgehammer. She lifted one corner of the pillow and squinted at the clock. Eight. It was only eight o'clock!

Muttering an oath, Mara threw back the sheet and snatched up the green satin robe from the end of the bed. Damn that Chuck! The idiot probably forgot his key! Her head swam dizzily as she made her way toward the door, and she held onto the wall for support. The aftereffects of the medication, combined with jet lag, had left her almost comatose.

Finally reaching the door, Mara fumbled with the lock and jerked it open. A shaft of brilliant sunlight hit her in the face; she flung one hand up to cover her eyes and slumped against the frame.

"Idiot! Imbecile! What the devil do you mean, waking me up at this ungodly hour?"

Thick silence greeted her words. Mara had expected a snappy comeback from Chuck. When none materialized she became uneasy. Very cautiously, she spread her fingers and peeked through them, straight into the coldest gray eyes she had ever seen; the eyes of a perfect stranger.

"Oh! I beg your pardon! I thought you were a friend of mine."

The man made no attempt to acknowledge her apology. "I'm looking for Mara Whitcomb," he stated coldly. Mara couldn't see his face clearly for the sun shining in her eyes, but the harsh clip to his voice and his tense stance conveyed his restless impatience.

"I'm Mara Whitcomb. What can I do for you?"

"You're the niece of the late Miss Enid Price?"

Mara's hand was cupped over her brow to shade her eyes from the glare. She rotated her thumb against her throbbing temple and tried to concentrate. "Uh . . . yes. That's right," she mumbled thickly.

His eyes ran over her tousled red hair and carefully inspected each sleep-softened feature before sweeping downward over the swell of her breasts and the lush curve of her hips to the bare toes peeping out beneath the hem of her robe.

Even with the sun at his back Mara couldn't miss the contemptuous curl of his lips as his eyes retraced their path back to her face. She felt the skin on the back of her neck crawl. No man had ever looked at her that way before. It was a distinctly new experience, and one she was sure she didn't want to repeat.

"Do you mind if I come in?" he asked pointedly. "I have a business proposition to discuss with you, in regard to the property you've inherited from your aunt, and I'd rather not do it on the doorstep."

"Oh! Of course." Mara stepped back and opened the door. "Won't you come in Mr. . . . uh . . . I'm sorry, I don't believe I caught your name."

"Grant Sloane." He stepped inside the foyer. As Mara closed the door he swung to face her, aggressive hostility crackling from him. "I've been trying to reach you by phone for weeks, but I kept getting that confounded recording. I left my name several times but you never bothered to return my calls, so I finally decided to come over here and talk to you in person. I'll come straight to the point. I want to purchase the property you inherited from your aunt."

Mara blinked. She was having trouble focusing her eyes and was so groggy she could barely think. What on earth was this overwhelming man babbling about? The room swayed alarmingly, and she put her hand on the newel-post to steady herself.

Grant Sloane stepped forward. "Are you ill?" He tilted his head to study her, his eyes narrowing. "Or just hung over?"

"No. No, I'm all right. It's just those darn pills. They always leave me feeling this way."

"Pills?" A look of utter revulsion crossed his face. "Oh, I see," he said, moving away from her.

Through the arched opening on her left Mara could see the living room. She seldom used it these days, but suddenly the elegantly furnished room looked very inviting. She gestured toward the door.

"Uh . . . would you like to come into the living room? We'll be more comfortable in there." The invitation was issued more from necessity than politeness. If he wanted to talk to her they had to sit down.

"No," he snapped harshly, and Mara looked up, surprised. "I have no intention of getting 'comfortable,' as you put it." His cold eyes flicked over her once again in obvious distaste. "This won't take long. The sooner I can get out of here the better." He ignored her startled expression and went on with hard determination. "Now, as I was saying, I want to purchase that forty acres, and I'm quite willing to pay whatever you ask."

"Bu—but . . . that property isn't for sale. And anyway, the contractor has already started building. I intend to move in just as soon as the house is completed."

Her vision had cleared somewhat, now that her eyes had adjusted to the dimmer light, and she stared at him openly. Mara saw people with an artist's eye, noting not only the overall picture but also all the minute details that make up the whole, things that ordinary people did not see—the way the sun-browned skin was stretched taut across the hard bones of his face, the aggressive, determined thrust to his square jaw, the eaglelike quality in those deep-set, piercing gray eyes. His hair was black and glossy, curling crisply over his ears and the back of his neck. His nose was straight and chiseled. The strong, austere planes of his face suggested strength of character and an unyielding nature. There was a hint of sensuality in the firm, controlled mouth, but it didn't have a softening effect. It was an impressive face, not really handsome in the conventional sense, but compelling and very, very male.

He was a powerfully built man, well over six feet tall, with broad shoulders and slender hips, and he exuded an air of potent masculinity that was almost primitive in its force. Yet, behind all that raw power, Mara sensed a gentleness, an absolute dependability. Grant Sloane was the kind of man who could always be relied on to take care of his own. Vaguely, Mara's mind registered the fact that he would be a very interesting subject to paint.

"Miss Whitcomb!" he snapped abruptly, bringing an end to her intent examination of his rugged features. The narrowed iciness of his eyes told her he had been aware of her inspection and had not liked it. "I am fully aware of the fact that building has already begun on the property, but I'm prepared to reimburse you on that score." His lips thinned. "Though, if you had answered my calls, that expense need not have been incurred."

"I'm sorry. I've been out of town," Mara explained, and was immediately irritated with herself for her apologetic tone. Who the devil did this man think he was? "Anyway, that's really beside the point. As I told you, Mr. Sloane, the property isn't for sale."

Grant Sloane's mouth twisted in scornful amusement, though his gray eyes remained cold. "Ah, but you haven't heard my offer yet."

He named a figure that left Mara speechless for a moment, her jaw dropping in astonishment.

She shook her head to clear it. Surely she hadn't heard him right. "But . . . I don't understand. That land isn't worth anywhere near that amount."

"It is to me," he stated unequivocally.

"But why?"

"The land is adjacent to my ranch. It will make a nice addition to my present holding."

Even in her dazed state Mara was not quite that gullible. She raked her fingers through the heavy tumble of bright hair, pushing it away from her face, and looked at him in exasperation. "Come now, Mr. Sloane. I may not be exactly with it this morning, but I'm not stupid. Even considering the high price of beef these days, it would take years just to recover your initial investment. You must have some other reason for wanting the property."

His eyes narrowed into two frosty slits and his fists clenched at his sides. It was obvious he had not expected her to question his motives. He had dangled the bait, thinking she would snap at it, and was furious that she had not.

Inexplicably, Mara felt a shiver of alarm feather up her spine.

"All right. Since you insist, I'll tell you. I want that land to keep you from moving onto it. I have no intention of having an immoral, unprincipled little tramp living practically on my doorstep," he snapped viciously, and Mara's head jerked back as though she'd been slapped. "I'm willing to pay whatever it takes to get rid of you, so just name your price."

Shock held her still for a moment, her clear green eyes wide and incredulous. Then fierce, hot anger began to bubble through her veins. Who the *hell* did he think he was? She didn't know this man. Until just a few minutes ago she had never even heard of him. And he certainly didn't know her! How *dare* he come in here and speak to her like that!

Fury stiffened Mara's spine and she drew herself up to her full height, tilting her chin at an aggressive angle, the debilitating dizziness of a few moments before forgotten.

"I told you, Mr. Sloane. The land is not for sale, but

even if it were, I wouldn't sell it to you. Not in a million years. I'm building a home on that property and I intend to move into it. If you find my presence so distasteful, then you can sell. I don't intend to.''

He stared at her, his face a tight, angry mask. ''Everything has its price,'' he stated flatly. His cold eyes ran over the fiery hair, then began a gradual descent over her face and figure. It was a calculated insult, and Mara's skin prickled in indignant reaction. ''If money holds no appeal for you perhaps we can work out another form of payment.'' He strolled toward her, smiling cruelly, and she took an instinctive step backward.

It suddenly hit her just how foolish she had been to let him in. She knew absolutely nothing about the man. She didn't even know if he was who he said he was. Stark, cold fear began to replace her earlier anger.

''Having trouble, love?''

Mara's knees went weak with relief as her eyes flew up to the stair landing, where Chuck stood looking down at them. He had evidently overheard a great deal. His normally friendly face was hard and stony as he returned Grant Sloane's challenging glare.

Chuck had been right last night when he'd said she wouldn't even know he was there. She hadn't.

He was barefoot and dressed in his usual painting garb of frayed cut-offs and a paint-splattered T-shirt. His sandy brown hair was tousled and unruly, making him look as though he'd just stumbled out of bed. As a knight in shining armor, Chuck was a ridiculous figure, but Mara didn't care. She had never been so happy to see anyone in her life!

Chuck wasn't as tall as Grant Sloane but he was more huskily built, broad shouldered and barrel chested, and rather bearlike. The other man's lean muscularity was impressive, but Mara suspected they would be evenly matched in a physical confrontation.

Drawing courage from Chuck's presence, Mara tightened the sash on her robe, walked to the door, and threw it open. "It's all right, Chuck. Mr. Sloane was just leaving."

If possible Grant Sloane's gray eyes grew even colder as they switched from Chuck to Mara, then back. His speculative gaze took in the other man's disheveled appearance, then traveled past him to the second-floor landing. "I'm terribly sorry," he sneered. "I didn't realize I was getting you two out of bed." He walked toward her, his insulting gaze running over Mara's body with disturbing thoroughness.

Over his shoulder, she caught a glimpse of Helen Thorn coming up the walk. Just as she reached the steps Grant turned around and delivered his parting shot.

"Though it beats me why any man would want to make love to a woman in your condition," he drawled hatefully.

Mara drew in a sharp, hissing breath. Before she could recover her voice he turned and stormed down the steps as though fleeing some vile contagion, brushing past the startled woman without a word.

Mara stared after him, her expression horrified. This person was going to be her neighbor? Good Lord! How on earth could she stand to live next door to such an obnoxious man? Suddenly, she realized that was exactly the reaction he had been trying to arouse. He had hoped to make her so angry, so uncomfortable, she would not even consider moving onto the property. Well, he could just go take a flying leap! It was her house, and she fully intended to live in it.

Helen's mouth had dropped open in astonishment, but she recovered quickly. Her eyes were twinkling with wry amusement as she walked into the foyer. "Well, now. What in the world was all that about?"

"Don't ask!" Mara slammed the door shut, turned, and stumbled down the hallway and into the kitchen. The swinging door hadn't had time to come to a stop before Helen pushed it open again. Chuck was right on her heels.

"Hey, now! This is Helen you're talking to. Remember? You can't expect me to come upon a scene like that and not ask questions."

Mara searched through the cabinet and found a glass, then filled it with water from the tap. She drank it down quickly, trying not to dwell on the hot fingers of pain inching their way up the back of her head. The migraine she had tried to avoid last night was catching up with her. She set the glass on the counter and turned to face her friend's inquisitive look.

"He's just some thoroughly objectionable man who's angry because I won't sell him that property I inherited from Enid."

"That forty acres up near Montgomery you're building your house on? How much did he offer you for it?" Helen asked, becoming suddenly businesslike.

Mara had to laugh in spite of her throbbing head. Helen was not only her friend but her accountant and business manager as well. There was nothing more guaranteed to grab her attention than the possibility of making a healthy profit.

"Good God!" Chuck's voice exploded over them in sudden wrath. "Didn't you hear the man? He insulted Mara! Not once, but several times! And all you can think about is turning a sharp deal. I've always known you had an adding machine for a heart, and you've just proved it."

Helen turned on him, snarling. "That's not true, Chuck Ainsley! Don't you dare say such a thing to me!"

"All right, you two. Knock it off, will you?" Mara intervened before a full-fledged battle could start. For some reason she had never been able to fully understand, Helen and Chuck could barely tolerate each other. Put them in the same room and they immediately squared off, circling one another like two dogs with their hackles up.

Helen smiled a rueful apology. "Anyway, if he was insulting it was probably just a case of sexual frustration." She twisted her mouth in mock disgust as her gaze roamed over Mara's beautifully disarrayed hair and slender body. "I mean, good grief! It ought to be against the law for anyone to be that gorgeous first thing in the morning."

Mara rolled her eyes and leaned back against the counter. Helen was the only close woman friend she had, and the only person who ever teased her about her looks. Most women were enviously distrustful of her flamboyant beauty. Helen had been too, at first, but their business relationship had thrown them together for prolonged periods, and she had soon been able to see beyond Mara's dazzling surface.

"Well, if he comes around here bothering Mara again he'll be suffering from more than frustration," Chuck inserted aggressively.

Helen flicked him an irritated look, then haughtily turned her back. "So tell me, how was the Paris show?" she asked, perching her petite body on a barstool next to the counter. She combed her fingers through her short black curls and then propped her chin in her hand, her pixielike face bright with curiosity.

"It was very well received. All in all, I was quite pleased," Mara replied, rubbing her temples distractedly.

"What Mara is saying, in her modest way, is it was a sellout," Chuck said teasingly.

"Hey! That's great! But then, I'm not surprised. The French do know their art." Helen pushed herself off the stool and picked up her purse from the kitchen table. "I'd love to hear more, but I'm afraid I have to run. I only stopped by to ask how the show went and to tell you I've been checking messages on your telephone answering machine and some man by the name of Grant Sloane has been calling you several times a day. From the messages he left, it sounded pretty urgent." Helen grinned and winked. "He sure has a sexy voice, honey. I'd get in touch with him if I were you. And if you don't want him, introduce him to me."

Mara gave her a baleful look. "I would have, but he practically knocked you down in his rush to get away," she said dryly.

"You mean *that* was Grant Sloane?" Mara's nod brought forth an exaggerated moan. "I knew he'd be gorgeous! I just *knew* it!"

A disdainful sniff was Mara's only response. Helen loved to make saucy comments like that, but they both knew she didn't mean them. She liked her life arranged in nice, tidy little compartments, with no surprises. Helen didn't take risks. She would run like a scalded cat if a man like Grant Sloane so much as looked at her.

Sighing mournfully, Helen walked toward the door. "By the way, when you get an accounting from the Paris gallery I'd like to go over it with you. I think you should invest most of the profits from this show. It would improve your tax picture considerably."

"There you go again," Chuck protested indignantly. "Profit and loss. That's all you ever think about. You're just about the most inhuman woman I've ever met!"

"I'm human enough to slap you silly if you keep that up," Helen snapped.

"You and whose army?" Chuck taunted back.

Usually Mara was amused by their ridiculous sparring. She assumed their mutual animosity was due to the vast differences in their personalities. Helen had a neat, orderly mind. She was cautious and well organized, in both her work and her personal life, while Chuck, though marvelously creative, tended to be rather harum-scarum. Helen abhorred his free-and-easy life-style, and he considered her to be cold and emotionless. They were like oil and water.

Mara felt the world spinning. She tried to close her ears

to the constant stream of bickering, but the excruciating pains shooting through her head made it impossible. Finally, she could stand it no longer.

"Children! Children! You'll have to continue your quarrel elsewhere. I can't take anymore."

Something in her voice got through to them. They turned to face her, wearing identically contrite expressions when they saw the pain-glazed look in her green eyes and the ghastly pallor of her skin.

"What is it, Mara?" Helen asked, hurrying back across the room to slip an arm around her waist. "Do you have a migraine?"

Unable to speak, Mara closed her eyes and nodded, instantly regretting the action.

Chuck hovered anxiously over them, a worried frown creasing his brow. Since David's death, two years earlier, these headaches had been occurring more and more frequently, and he and Helen both knew how devastating they could be.

"Do you want me to get your tablets?"

"No!" Mara gasped. "They wouldn't do any good now. I wouldn't be able to keep them down."

Helen and Chuck exchanged a look of silent communication. Helen nodded her head and murmured, "I'll go call the doctor," as Chuck swept Mara up in his arms and headed for the bedroom.

Chapter Two

"What do you want me to load next?" Chuck asked.

Mara straightened up from the box she had been filling with books. She was clad in a pair of denim shorts and a halter top, and her hair was drawn away from her face in one thick plait that hung down her back to a point between her shoulder blades, yet perspiration still beaded her face. She patted it away with the back of her hand and sighed heavily.

"Well, I guess the next thing should be the canvases. I've sorted the ones I want to take with me. They're up in the studio, leaning against the wall to the right of the door."

"Sure thing." Chuck pivoted on his heel and started for the stairs.

"Oh, Chuck!" Mara called after him, rushing to the arched opening between the entry and the living room. "Be sure to place a quilted pad between each painting and the next. There's a stack of pads in the storeroom."

Chuck had already reached the first landing when Mara's voice stopped him. He looked down at her in affectionate exasperation, shaking his shaggy head. "Now would I take chances with the work of a genius? I've helped pack your paintings for shipment before, you know."

Chastened, Mara gave him a sheepish look. "Sorry. I do get a trifle paranoid about them, don't I?"

He laughed softly. "Don't worry about it, love. If they were mine, I'd be a blithering idiot if anyone so much as touched them." He winked and continued up the stairs, whistling happily.

A tender smile softened Mara's face as she returned to the half-filled carton. She was lucky to have two friends like Chuck and Helen. If it hadn't been for their concern and support during the past two years she would have gone quietly out of her mind. Chuck had absorbed the angry backlash of her grief with unshakable amiability. He had seen her through the inevitable stages: shock, disbelief, the irrational feeling of rejection, anger, and then, ultimately, painful, painful acceptance and despair. Many times she had lashed out at him in frustration, but he had remained steadfast, his friendship firm and unbreakable.

If Chuck had been her cushion, Helen had been her lifeline. She was brisk and matter-of-fact. She had been compassionate and understanding but had absolutely refused to allow Mara to sink into the pit of black depression that had beckoned to her. Helen's no-nonsense attitude had forced Mara to pay attention to details and get on with the business of living, one day at a time.

Work had been a great panacea, but even she could not paint every waking moment. Somehow, between the two of them, Helen and Chuck had seen to it that she was never alone for very long periods of time. Mara picked up another book and carefully dusted it before placing it in the carton with the others, her mouth tilting in a wry smile. It had been a conspiracy, plain and simple, and it had probably been the only thing on which Helen and Chuck had agreed in all the years they'd known one another.

"I think I'm all done in the kitchen," Helen announced, strolling into the room and wiping her hands on the seat of her jeans. "Everything is packed and ready. As soon as Chuck loads it all, and the rest in here, we'll be ready to leave."

"Fine." Mara's eyes were sad as they wandered around the room, lingering on the pale aqua wallpaper and the cream-painted woodwork, then automatically skimming over the complimenting aqua, cream and pale peach Aubusson rug. All the colors in the house were soft and muted, carefully chosen by David to enhance her vivid coloring.

Seeing Mara's expression, Helen asked gently, "Are you sure you really want to make this move? You don't have to, you know. The house and property in Montgomery could be sold." She looked around the room in open admiration. "This place is so perfect. I don't know how you can bear to leave it."

"That's just the point, Helen. It is perfect. And everything about it reminds me of David. Everywhere I look, everything I touch, brings back some poignant memory. I don't think there's a single ashtray or lampshade we didn't choose together." Mara placed the last book in the carton and closed the lid. "It's been two years, Helen, and I'm still hurting. I've finally come to the conclusion that I always will as long as I live here with all these memories."

Her eyes circled the room once again and she recalled the night they had hung the wallpaper. They hadn't used enough paste, and as soon as the final strip was hung on the ceiling the whole thing had come slithering down on

top of them. Most of it had fallen on David, and he had
looked like some monster in a science fiction movie as he
fought his way out of the sticky mass, cursing eloquently.
She had dissolved in a fit of giggles. "Oh-ho! You think
it's funny, do you?" he had growled ferociously, and in
retaliation had chased her down and tickled her unmercifully. They had ended up making love on the floor, amid
all the mess and debris . . . and it had been wonderful.

With painful determination, Mara dragged her mind
away from the past. No. She couldn't stay here. She had to
build a new life for herself, a life where David didn't exist
as he existed here, if only in phantom memories.

"Yes, perhaps you're right," Helen agreed sadly. "But
I hate for you to move so far away."

"Heavens! It's not that far! Anyway, I'll be in town
frequently, and you can visit me anytime you like."

"But it won't be the same."

"No, Helen, it won't," Mara agreed quietly. "And
that's another reason for leaving. I've become too depen-
dent on you and Chuck, and I've taken up too much of
your time. You both have your own lives to lead and you'll
have more time to do that, now that you don't have to
baby-sit with me."

"That's the biggest bunch of nonsense I've ever
heard!" Helen began angrily, but Mara held up her hands
and cut her off.

"No, Helen. I mean it. And if you'll just think about it
you'll know I'm right. Now, I don't want to argue about
it. The matter is settled."

A battle of conflicting emotions was reflected in
Helen's expression, a tug of war between her common
sense and her heart. It was unfortunate that Chuck chose
that moment to amble into the room.

"Okay, what's next?" he asked, blissfully unaware of
the tension between the two women, and immediately
became the target for Helen's helpless frustration.

"Oh, for heaven's sake! Do we have to tell you everything?" she snapped.

"What did *I* do?" he protested indignantly.

Helen threw him a withering look and stalked toward the door. "Well, come on. There are plenty of boxes out in the kitchen to be loaded."

Bewildered, Chuck turned to Mara and spread his hands wide in a palms-up, helpless gesture, then turned and followed Helen out of the room.

Slightly over an hour later, with everything piled into Chuck's van and the trunk and back seat of Mara's car, they reached the small town of Montgomery. Leading the way, Mara turned off onto a little-used farm road and continued on another two miles before turning into the narrow drive that led to the newly constructed house. For privacy, she'd had it built in a small clearing, out of sight of the road. It was an oversized A-frame made of rough-cut cedar, with large expanses of glass. To Mara's delight, it seemed to nestle into its surroundings as though it had always been there.

It was an informal house, as different from her home in Houston as night and day. A large living room ran the entire depth of the structure. One wall was dominated by a massive stone fireplace, and in the back corner there was a small, gleaming kitchen, separated from the living room only by an L-shaped counter. To the left, opening off the living room, was a large master bedroom and bath, and beyond that, a smaller bedroom for overnight guests. A stairway ran up the wall opposite the fireplace, leading to a spacious loft that extended out over half the downstairs area. Here was Mara's studio. The north wall, which was also the eave of the roof, was a huge triangle of glass. In each side of the steeply slanted ceiling a large skylight flooded the loft with soft, diffused light.

The decor of the entire house was rustic, leaning toward country French, with massive, dark beams and chintz-covered furniture. Everything was new, except the few personal things Mara had brought with her. This was a new start, in a new home, and she wanted nothing to remind her of what she'd had . . . and lost.

"It's beautiful, Mara," Helen murmured as she wandered aimlessly around the living room. She trailed her hand along the back of the blue-and-white print sofa and let her eyes wander over the dark blue chairs and the stark white walls. "But isn't it a little . . ."—her gaze switched to the wide expanse of glass across the front of the room and beyond to the towering pines that surrounded the clearing—"remote?"

"For heaven's sake, Helen! I told you it was in the country. What did you expect?"

"Well, certainly not this!" Helen snapped crossly. "You'll turn into a hermit out here. Why, there's not another living soul in sight. And I'd bet my last dollar there's not an eligible male in the whole county." Helen paced back and forth across the floor, her hands in the hip pockets of her jeans, growing more agitated by the second.

With a sigh, Mara sank down onto the arm of the sofa. "So. We're back to that again, are we? I've told you, Helen, I'm simply not ready for that sort of thing yet."

"When will you be ready?" Helen probed relentlessly.

Mara looked at her, distress evident in her tormented expression. She shook her head, fighting back tears, and Helen's face softened. "I . . . I just don't know. Maybe never." She turned and looked out through the glass wall, her face pensive. "Whoever said 'It's better to have loved and lost than never to have loved at all' was a fool."

"Now you're beginning to sound like your Aunt Enid," Helen snapped, making no attempt to hide her disgust.

Mara shrugged. "I didn't agree with her on most things, but she was right about love. It's a painful, destructive emotion. You of all people should know that."

"You mean because my husband left me for another woman?" Helen's smile was wry and a trifle bitter. "Oh, I'll admit that hurt. It hurt like hell. But I got over it. Don't let this starchy exterior fool you, honey. If I ever again meet a man I can love, who will love me back, I'm going to grab him with both hands."

"Which only proves you're braver than I." Mara bit her lip as the familiar tightness squeezed at her chest. Until David, there had been precious little love in her life. Against her will, memories of her coldly handsome father crowded in, and her face suddenly grew hard. When his ex-wife died Ray Kendall had dutifully accepted financial responsibility for his daughter, but that had been as far as his paternal feelings would stretch. Her boarding-school fees had been paid promptly and she had been provided with a generous allowance and an extravagant wardrobe, but of her father Mara saw next to nothing. Silent, bitter laughter rose in Mara's throat as she thought of those lonely, unhappy years. Oh, no, Ray Kendall couldn't be saddled with a gangly, teenage daughter. That would definitely have put a damper on his active social life. The sticky problem of what to do with her during holidays and vacations was solved by simply paying Enid Price, his ex-wife's sister, to take her. Enid had been quite willing to do almost anything for money.

Enid. Mara's bitterness deepened as she thought of her selfish, totally amoral aunt. Had her father known what Enid was like when he consigned her to the woman's far from tender care? Had it even mattered to him? Not that Enid had mistreated her. She had simply been indifferent. Being an artist herself, Enid had insisted that Mara's natural talents be developed. Beyond that, her aunt had shown no interest in her at all.

Enid had been livid when Mara had fallen head over heels in love with David and they had announced their engagement. "Sleep with him, if you must," her aunt had snapped. "I have nothing against sex. But for God's sake, don't tie yourself down to one man! Love is an illusion only a fool would believe in. It never lasts, and when it's over you'll suffer, and so will your work."

But Mara had not listened to her. She and David had married on her twenty-first birthday. For five years they had been blissfully happy. During that time David's law practice had flourished, and Mara's reputation as an artist had grown to the point where she could no longer accept all the commissions that came her way. They had been the envy of all their friends: attractive, successful, and deeply in love. And then, just as Mara had begun to relax and accept her happiness, it had ended, with devastating suddenness.

Mara stood up and walked to the glass wall. A bushy-tailed squirrel, who had been busily investigating the front deck, leaped to the ground and scampered away. She watched it go with troubled eyes. "It's no use, Helen. Call me a coward if you like, but I'm not anxious to expose myself to that kind of hurt again."

"Hey, Mara! This studio is great!"

Mara turned and saw Chuck standing at the loft railing. She smiled, grateful for the interruption. "Thanks. Feel free to use it any time."

"I may just do that. So make sure that guest bed has a good mattress."

The serious mood was shattered. After flinging Mara one last, exasperated look, Helen started toward the door. "All right, come on, you two," she commanded briskly. "There's plenty of work to do."

Chuck groaned and came loping down the stairs two at a time. "Slave driver. Work, work, work. My God, woman! Don't you ever think of anything else?"

Helen's brown eyes flashed fire. She gave him a scorching look that should have singed the hair from his head. "No. That's not all I think of, Chuck Ainsley! But at least it's better than jumping into bed with every charming, witless bit of fluff that comes along." Her mouth curled scornfully, her eyes flicking over his huge body as though the sight of it offended her. "It's about time you put all that excess energy to some constructive use."

"What the hell would you know about it?" Chuck snarled, coming to a thumping halt at the bottom of the stairs. He bent over, thrusting his large, shaggy head forward menacingly. "At least those 'charming bits of fluff' are warm, loving women. Not some heartless little icicle like . . ."

The knock on the door halted Chuck's furious tirade, and three startled faces turned toward the sound. A casual caller was the last thing they had expected in this secluded spot. Recovering first, Mara started for the door, silently blessing whoever was on the other side. Despite Chuck's accusations, she could see that Helen was anything but cool. She had been building up a full head of steam in defense against his taunts, and if someone hadn't put a stop to it, their petty little quarrel would have escalated into an all-out donnybrook. It's strange, Mara thought as she pulled the door open, Chuck was both right and wrong. Helen *was* cool . . . with everyone but him, a phenomenon that seemed to escape both of them.

"Vicky!"

"Hi, Mara. I was out riding"—the girl gestured behind her to the chestnut mare tied to a tree at the edge of the clearing—"and saw the van and car. I figured you were probably moving in, so I thought I'd stop by and see if I could be of any help." She smiled shyly, her blue eyes flickering with uncertainty.

Smiling, Mara reached out and drew her inside. "Of course you can. Another strong back is always welcome.

And I'd like you to meet my friends." Mara felt the younger girl's instinctive withdrawal as she caught sight of Helen and Chuck but urged her forward with a firm hand against her back.

Mara quickly made the introductions, a warning glitter in her eyes when she smiled at the two combatants. Before she had finished, Chuck's face lit up with recognition.

"Of course! This is the girl you've been sketching."

Vicky blushed painfully, and Mara smiled. She was such a shy creature. It was a rare quality in a young girl these days. From her looks Mara judged her to be about eighteen or nineteen, but her timid manner made her appear much younger. Vicky had come riding up on her horse one day, about a month before, while Mara had been inspecting the building site. She had introduced herself rather timidly and welcomed Mara to the area, explaining that she lived nearby. After that she had appeared regularly whenever Mara came to check the progress on the house, and despite the girl's almost painful shyness, a tentative friendship had sprung up between them. There was an elusive quality about Vicky that had drawn Mara from the very beginning, a sad wistfulness that touched an answering chord deep inside her.

"Yes," Mara said, confirming Chuck's statement. "So far I've only done a few preliminary sketches, but Vicky has agreed to pose for me, once I get settled in here." A panic-stricken look flickered across Vicky's face, and Mara laughed, squeezing her arm gently. "Don't fret. It will be painless. I promise."

Vicky was tall and willowy, with long, silky blond hair and the softest blue eyes Mara had ever seen. She wanted to capture that wistfulness on canvas and had been toying with several different poses, but she hadn't decided on anything definite as yet.

"Honey, you don't know how lucky you are." Chuck

treated Vicky to one of his lazy smiles. "There are people waiting in line, willing to pay Mara a great deal of money just for the privilege of having her paint them."

Vicky's big blue eyes widened. "Really? Are you famous?"

Mara shot Chuck an annoyed look and shrugged. "Somewhat," she hedged.

"If we're going to get this job done today I suggest we get at it," Helen inserted, steering them toward the stacks of boxes cluttering the living room. "The sooner we get this mess sorted, the sooner Mara can get started on Vicky's portrait. Then she can judge for herself just how good Mara is."

For the next few hours they worked like beavers. While Chuck hauled in her painting supplies and set up her new studio easel, Mara arranged the kitchen to her satisfaction, and Helen and Vicky unpacked linens and odds and ends. Even with four people working, it took all afternoon to complete the unpacking. By the time the paintings were hung and all the cartons were emptied, they were exhausted and almost giddy with hunger.

Helen collapsed onto the sofa, stretching out full length. "Oooohh, my back! I never realized moving was such hard work," she groaned.

"Forget your back. It's my stomach I'm worried about." Chuck resembled a huge bear, sprawled on the rug in front of the fireplace, one arm flung up over his eyes. "Food! I need food!" he wailed pitifully. "If I don't eat soon I won't have the strength to drive back to town."

Laughing, Mara hauled herself up out of the chair she had fallen into. "All right, all right. I can take a hint." She smiled at Vicky. "These two like their steaks medium rare. How about you?"

"Oh, really? I . . . I don't think I'd better . . ." she

stammered and started to rise, but Mara stopped her with a hand on her shoulder.

"Nonsense. You worked just as hard as the rest of us. And besides, we want you to stay. Now you just sit right there and rest, and I'll get started."

The cooler containing most of the perishable food items was still in the trunk of Mara's car. She was bending over it, rummaging around for four steaks, when she heard the sound of a vehicle coming up the drive.

The pickup came to a stop a few feet behind Mara as she slammed the trunk lid and turned around. At first she didn't recognize the man behind the wheel, but when he climbed from the cab and started toward her with that lazy, loping walk something jogged her memory, and her eyes widened in surprise.

She hadn't seen Grant Sloane in over three months. She hadn't even given him a thought. For a few days after his visit she had been troubled by his hostility. It was obvious the man had a low opinion of her but, for the life of her, she couldn't figure out why. She had received one terse letter from his attorney, raising the offer for her property to a ridiculous amount. Her prompt reply had been a very firm, very definite no, and she had heard no more from him. Within a short time she had put the matter completely out of her mind.

Grant's gaze went beyond her to where the pile of empty cartons lay strewn over the front deck. "I see you've moved in." It was a cold statement, containing not a vestige of warmth or welcome.

Mara's chin lifted. "Was there something you wanted, Mr. Sloane?" She had not been operating at peak efficiency the morning they met, but even so, she could still recall the insults he had hurled at her. The cold clip to his voice told her his opinion hadn't changed.

Grant's eyes ran over the bare skin exposed by the

flimsy halter top, down over the silky smoothness of her midriff to the skimpy denim shorts, and continued along the long, shapely legs in unhurried appraisal. There was not a spark of appreciation in his eyes—just hard, frigid contempt.

"I've come to collect my sister," he grated harshly.

"Your sister?" Mara blinked. Whatever she had expected him to say, that was not it. "I'm afraid I don't understand."

"Don't play dumb, Miss Whitcomb," he snapped. "And don't try to deny that she's here, because it won't work. That's her horse right over there."

Mara's head swung toward the big chestnut cropping grass at the edge of the clearing, then back to the angry man in front of her. Her emerald green eyes were wide with shock. "Vicky is *your* sister?" She couldn't believe it! That shy, gentle girl was related to this man? It didn't seem possible. And there was no family resemblance at all.

"Yes."

"Bu—but . . . her name is . . ."

"Ridgeway. To be precise, she's my half-sister, but that's beside the point," he said with growing impatience. "Now where is she?"

"I'm here, Grant."

Surprised, Mara swung around in time to see Vicky hurrying down the steps, her expression worried and apprehensive.

"You're wanted at home, Vicky," her brother stated tersely.

"Oh, but . . ."

"I said you're wanted at home." He paused and waited for her to move. When she didn't, he barked, "Now!" and she jumped, then scurried away toward her horse.

Mara stood watching the whole thing in wide-eyed

disbelief. She slanted a sidelong look at Grant. He was
watching Vicky through narrowed eyes, his head thrown
back, his black brows drawn together above his arrogant
nose. Oh, you really are a charming man, she thought,
fuming.

"I'm sorry I can't stay for dinner, Mara," Vicky said
softly when she had climbed into the saddle. "But thank
you for the invitation. Perhaps I can come back tomorrow,
if you'd like to get started on that portrait."

Mara caught her brother's start of surprise and shot him
a defiant glare. "That will be fine, Vicky," she said,
smiling stiffly. She was seething over his dictatorial
attitude, but if Vicky wasn't going to make any effort to
stand up to him, she certainly wasn't going to fight her
battles for her.

A heavy silence hung between Mara and Grant as they
watched her ride away toward the back of the house and
disappear through the trees.

"What the hell was that business about a portrait?"

Mara turned her head and gave him a haughty look.
"Vicky's going to pose for me," she said matter-of-factly
and waited for the explosion to come. When she had asked
Vicky to pose she'd had no idea the girl was Grant's
sister. If she had, she wouldn't have bothered, because it
was a sure bet he wasn't going to allow it.

"*What!*" The word shot out of him like a bullet. "Like
hell she is!" he roared. He stepped closer, his face livid
with rage. "You listen to me, Miss Whitcomb. My sister
is a sweet, unspoiled innocent, and she's going to stay that
way. If you think I'm going to allow her to become
involved with you and your friends, think again. For the
short time you'll be here, you're to stay away from my
sister. Do I make myself clear?"

Mara glared back at him. "Perfectly, as far as your
sister is concerned. But you'd better explain that bit about
'the short time I'll be here.' I thought I had explained to

you that this is to be my home. As of today, I'm a permanent resident.''

Grant didn't answer immediately, but his taunting expression made her uneasy. He reached into his shirt pocket and extracted a cigarette with two fingers. Flicking his lighter, he cupped the flame to the tip, squinting his eyes against the sudden flare. She watched him inhale, then blow a stream of blue smoke upward. In that instant Mara knew he was deliberately making her wait for an answer, trying his best to anger her. When she didn't react, he raised one black brow.

A cynical grin split his face. ''Somehow I doubt that,'' he said mockingly, flicking the gray ash from the tip of his cigarette. ''I think you'll soon discover that life here is far too simple for your taste. There are no bright lights, no discos, no entertainment of any kind, other than visiting friends and an occasional barbecue. Within a month you'll be out of your head with boredom,'' he stated nastily. ''And if you've any ideas of importing your own entertainment, let me give you a little advice, a neighborly warning, if you like. This is a simple rural community, made up of decent, upstanding people who have no use for the 'new morality.' '' His voice deepened and hardened. ''Pot parties and that sort of thing won't be tolerated.''

Mara stared at him, amazed. Despite her irritation, she almost laughed aloud at his ludicrous assertions. Pot parties? *Her?* Is that what he thought she'd be doing here in this lovely, secluded place? Why, she didn't even drink! And the only drug she had ever taken was the migraine medication she was forced to use at times. He was obviously one of those people who thought of an artist as some kind of degenerate.

Her eyes glittered like two jewels, but Mara bit back the stinging retort that tingled on her tongue. You couldn't fight prejudice. What good did it do? And anyway, why should she? This man meant nothing to her. Let him think what he liked. She gave him a cool, unruffled smile. "Thank you for your advice, Mr. Sloane. I shall remember that."

He hadn't expected that, she could tell. He seemed stunned, and Mara felt a smug sense of satisfaction at the disconcerted look that flickered across his face. Her calm, dignified manner had thrown him; it didn't fit his preconceived idea of her as a . . . what was it he'd called her before? . . . an immoral, unprincipled little tramp? Mara suppressed the malicious little smile that tugged at the corners of her mouth. This arrogant, opinionated man was in for a few surprises. Eventually the truth would dawn on him. Only a fool could ignore the obvious indefinitely, and although she found him thoroughly irritating, she didn't think he was a fool. But she certainly wasn't going to enlighten him.

Feeling more in control, Mara relaxed, and automatically her artist's training took over, her sharp gaze tracing the hard-boned face with its cleanly chiseled features, her intent scrutiny totally analytical, impersonal. His expression tightened under the close inspection, but Mara's absorption was complete and his irritation didn't register.

He certainly is a marvelous male specimen, she thought abstractedly. If Helen thought he was gorgeous before, she should see him now.

The first time Mara had seen Grant he'd been wearing a suit and tie and had been the picture of the polished, in-control business man. His potent brand of masculinity had been evident even then, but it paled beside the aura he exuded now. The civilized trappings were gone, exposing the untamed animal, big and tough and exceedingly dangerous. A faded western-style shirt was stretched taut over his deep-muscled chest, the sleeves rolled up to expose brawny forearms covered with a liberal sprinkling of short, dark hair. Soft, well-worn jeans molded lean hips and muscular thighs like a second skin. The battered, dusty cowboy boots proclaimed him to be a working rancher, not just a figurehead.

It occurred to Mara that Chuck's advertising agency would love him. He could easily star in one of those ads where the silent, flinty-eyed, macho type rides his horse off into the sunset. The ridiculous thought caused her lips to twitch with amusement.

"Do you find the situation funny, Miss Whitcomb?" Grant demanded tautly.

"What? Oh!" Mara's eyes snapped back into focus. "No. No, of course not. I was thinking of something el—"

"Where's my dinner, woman! I'm starving!" Chuck bellowed from the house, and Mara jumped.

Grant's silvery gray eyes narrowed dangerously. "So. Your boyfriend has moved in with you." He gave her a scathing look that made her feel like something that had crawled out from under a rock. "I hope he's the understanding type. If you were my woman and you'd looked at another man the way you just looked at me, I'd probably strangle you."

"What!" Mara couldn't let that go by. "Now just wait one minute, Mr. Sloane! In the first place, I'm no man's woman. Chuck is a friend of mine. Full stop! He and another friend have been helping me move. And in the second place, I wasn't—"

"Save your breath, Miss Whitcomb. I'm really not interested," Grant interrupted in a hateful, bored voice. The half-smoked cigarette was dropped and crushed under his heel; then he pivoted toward the pickup. He had climbed in behind the wheel, pulled the door shut, and started the engine before Mara recovered from her astonishment.

Hooking an arm over the window opening, he gave her a sardonic smile. "Just remember what I told you. And when you get tired of the quiet life, let me know. I'll be glad to take this place off your hands.'' Mara simply gazed in stupefaction as he put the truck in gear and accelerated down the drive.

Chuck was standing at the door when she climbed the steps to the front deck. ''What the hell was that all about?'' he demanded. ''I was just coming to find out what was taking so long when I saw that Sloane fellow drive away.''

''Just more of the same. A few insults, along with another offer to buy this place.''

Chuck followed her into the kitchen, scowling like a black thundercloud. ''Now see here, Mara. I don't like the idea of leaving you out here alone, with that guy so close by.''

Mara calmly unwrapped the steaks and placed them on a broiler pan. The unpleasant encounter with her hostile neighbor had unsettled her. It seemed a bad omen, casting a shadow on the new life she was trying to build for herself. But she had no intention of allowing Helen or Chuck to see how much the man's insults had bothered her. They were worried enough about her already.

''Don't be silly, Chuck. I'll grant you, the man is thoroughly obnoxious, but I doubt he's violent. I just discovered that he's Vicky's half brother, so he can't be all bad. Anyway, I probably won't be seeing much of him. I intend to avoid him like the plague, and I doubt he'll be dropping by for a neighborly visit.'' She sprinkled the steaks with seasoning and set them aside before turning to the refrigerator.

''Well, maybe so,'' Chuck conceded grudgingly. ''But I still don't like it.''

Helen wandered over to the dividing bar and perched herself on a stool. She propped an elbow on the counter and cupped her chin in her hand, eyeing Mara with a speculative look. ''Is he single?'' she asked with feigned innocence.

"What the hell does that have to do with anything?" Chuck demanded irritably.

Mara turned from the refrigerator with her arms full of salad ingredients and gave Helen a long-suffering look. "Ignore her, Chuck," she instructed dryly. "Helen's got this insane notion that what I need most in the world is a husband, and she's hell-bent on matchmaking."

Chuck's first reaction was a startled "What!" But to Mara's amazement, the stunned look faded rapidly and a thoughtful, serious one took its place. "You know, now that I think of it, that's not such a bad idea."

"I don't believe this!" Mara dumped the vegetables into the sink and planted her hands on her hips. Throwing her head back, she gazed at the ceiling, as though seeking guidance from above. "Now listen, you two," she began threateningly as she took in the bland, innocent expressions. "Just knock it off. I'm not interested in acquiring another husband at the moment, but even if I were, that Grant Sloane person would definitely not be a candidate. Good grief! The man despises me!"

"Oh, that's probably just sexual antagonism." Helen airily dismissed Mara's protest. "It often happens when two people are strongly attracted to one another."

Mara fixed them both with a hard stare. "In that case, you two must be madly in love."

There was a stunned silence, followed quickly by a barrage of protest. In the ensuing argument, Grant Sloane was forgotten.

Chapter Three

After the initial strangeness wore off, Mara settled into her new home with ease. Within a few weeks her days began to fall into a pattern that was both productive and relaxing. She awoke early every morning in a sunlit room to the sound of birds twittering outside her window and the audacious chattering of squirrels as they chased each other from branch to branch. Most mornings Mara ate her breakfast on the back deck. As she sipped her coffee, she also drank in the peace and quiet, the absolute serenity of the place. It was a different quiet from that she'd known in her Houston suburb—more natural. There you were always aware that just a few short blocks away there was a city, packed with people and pulsing with life. Here the quiet was an intrinsic part of the surroundings, like the trees and the animals. Yet, strangely, the solitude didn't bother Mara. It hurt worse, somehow, to be alone in a city full of people.

After breakfast, Mara painted, taking only a short break

at midday for a quick bite, then continuing straight through until the afternoon, when she lost the light. Then, armed with sketch pad and pencil, she roamed the woods. The forty acres of unspoiled land contained an endless variety of subjects to paint, and Mara quickly filled pad after pad.

Helen and Chuck had driven out together one Sunday, which had surprised her. For some strange reason, they had seemed nervous and ill at ease and, after only a few hours, had returned to the city. Their behavior puzzled Mara and she wondered if the complete isolation bothered their city-bred souls.

Of Vicky and her brother she had seen nothing since the day she moved in, but that didn't surprise Mara. She was quite sure Grant had laid down the law to his young sister, and though Vicky was of age, she was evidently too timid to defy him.

Not that Mara wanted her to. She had no intention of being drawn into a family squabble. As much as she wanted to paint Vicky, it simply wasn't worth it, and she resigned herself to the fact that their budding friendship had come to an end. Which was why she was so surprised to find Vicky waiting for her one day as she tramped through the woods.

"Vicky! How nice to see you," Mara exclaimed when she entered a small clearing and saw the girl sitting on a rock next to a placid stream. She had been sitting with her chin propped on her drawn-up knees, her expression morose, but at the sound of Mara's voice she looked up and smiled.

"Hi, Mara." Vicky stood up slowly. Her eyes flickered with embarrassment, and a tide of pink color flooded her cheeks. "I'm sorry I haven't been over to pose as I promised, but you see . . ." Her voice faltered and she dropped her gaze. With the toe of one boot she traced circles round and round in the soft sand of the creek bank. Her eyes followed the circles with intense concentration. "Well, the truth is . . ."

"Don't worry about it, Vicky," Mara said softly. "I do understand."

The younger girl looked up, her brow puckered. "Do you?"

"Oh, yes. Your brother has made his feelings quite plain."

Vicky sighed. "I'm sorry, Mara. I don't know what's the matter with Grant. I know you'll find this hard to believe, but he's usually a fair man. That's why his attitude is so baffling. He won't even allow your name to be mentioned, especially in my mother's hearing. I just don't understand it."

"Neither do I, but don't worry about it. I don't blame you."

Mara sat down on a large rock and flipped back the cover on her sketch pad. With swift, sure strokes she began to sketch the little stream winding through the forest and the big chestnut horse grazing contentedly beside its bank. Her eyes flickered back and forth between her subject and the rapidly emerging picture, her hand moving constantly. "There's another thing I don't understand, Vicky," Mara said quietly, her concentration never wavering. "Since your brother has made his feelings so clear, what are you doing here? I'm quite sure he wouldn't approve."

"No, he wouldn't. And I did promise Grant that I wouldn't pose for you." Vicky spread her hands in a helpless gesture. "He seems to think you'd expect me to pose nude, or close to it, anyway."

Mara looked up, her delicate brows arched in surprise. "Does he, indeed?" She smiled and turned back to the drawing, thinking with amusement of the lovely, wistful painting she had intended to do of Vicky. The man was certainly good at jumping to conclusions.

"But I *do* like you, Mara, and I'd like to be your friend," Vicky said earnestly. "I see no harm in just talking to you and enjoying your company occasionally. Grant need never know."

Mara's hand halted. "Oh, Vicky. I don't think . . ."

"Please, Mara. I need someone to talk to. Someone young. At the ranch there's only my mother, Grant, and our housekeeper, Mrs. Booker, who's at least fifty. There's absolutely no one who understands how I feel," she wailed.

The youthful intensity of her complaint brought a smile to Mara's lips. Even so, she felt herself weakening. She was tempted to point out that there was at least ten years' difference in their ages but didn't. The desperate entreaty in those soft blue eyes was just too much for her. There was something making this young girl terribly unhappy, something she obviously needed to share with someone, and although Mara knew she was probably asking for trouble, she simply could not deny Vicky's request. Sighing, Mara put down her pencil and looked up into Vicky's anxious eyes. "Okay. But I'm probably out of my mind to agree to this. Your brother will tear strips off me when he finds out." She stopped and gave Vicky a stern look. "Which he's bound to do, sooner or later. You do realize that, don't you?"

Vicky grimaced. "I know, I know. He'll be hopping mad." She frowned, then suddenly jutted out her small, rounded chin. "Well, I don't care! I'm not going to give in on this. Grant is being unreasonable and totally unfair!"

Mara smiled and picked up her pencil. Perhaps there was a little healthy rebellion in the girl after all.

During the next hour they talked sporadically while Mara sketched. Vicky watched, fascinated by the ease with which Mara could transform a blank page into a lovely scene with just a few quick strokes of the pencil. Their conversation covered a variety of topics, all of them impersonal, both women cautiously testing the water before revealing anything of a private nature.

Around six o'clock Mara folded her sketch pad and stood up. She raised her arms above her head and stretched, easing the tight muscles in her back. Although it was late September, it was still hot, especially there, deep in the woods where little breeze stirred. Mara bent her arm behind her and with her thumb and forefinger pulled the sweat-dampened shirt away from her back.

"Phew! It's hot. If that stream were just a little deeper I'd be tempted to go skinny-dipping."

"I've got a better idea," Vicky said quickly. "Why don't you come home with me and go for a swim in our pool?"

Mara shot her a surprised look. "You know I can't do that! Your brother would have a conniption."

"Sure you can," Vicky assured her. "Mother is spending a week with her sister in Tulsa, and Grant went into Houston this morning on business. He won't be back until tomorrow. So we'll have the whole place to ourselves. Please say you'll come. It's no fun swimming alone."

"Well . . ." Mara knew she should refuse the invitation outright. If Grant ever found out about it he'd be livid. Still, the thought of a swim *was* tempting. Surely it wouldn't hurt . . . just for a little while.

"Come on, Mara," Vicky urged. "We'll go by your house for your swim suit and you can ride behind me on Dolly. It's just about a mile to our place if you follow the old deer trail through the woods. If we hurry we'll have plenty of time to swim before dark."

Mara executed a neat dive off the low board, touched bottom, then thrust upward. She broke the surface laughing and trod water while she smoothed back the wet mane of fiery hair. Green eyes sparkled between spiky wet lashes. She smiled at Vicky, who was lying propped against the edge of the pool. "This is great! I'm glad I let you talk me into it," she said breathlessly, moving forward with a smooth, powerful breast stroke. When she reached Vicky's side Mara curled her fingers around the concrete lip of the pool. Turning her back against the side, she stretched her arms out over the edge and let her legs float out languorously in the gently bobbing water. With eyes closed, she savored the sensation.

"Mmmmm, this could get to be habit-forming. I'll have to give serious consideration to putting in a pool at my place."

"If Grant would just stop being so pigheaded you could swim here with me every day." Vicky sighed disconsolately.

"Don't hold your breath." Mara could just imagine how he'd react to that suggestion!

"You know," Vicky mused, "Grant's attitude really puzzles me. I think it must stem from the fact that you're an artist."

Mara turned her head and looked at her. "What does that have to do with anything? Does he have something against art?"

"No, it's not that. But you see, his father left Mother for another woman when Grant was just fifteen, and she was an artist."

A tiny chill ran up Mara's spine. Inexplicably, she was filled with a sense of foreboding. "Do you know the woman's name?" she asked quietly, dreading the answer.

"Yes. Her name was Enid Price."

Shock held Mara rigid, but Vicky was looking straight ahead over the surface of the pool and didn't notice Mara's strained expression.

"The sad part is, the woman didn't want him, at least

not on a permanent basis. But he didn't find that out until it was too late. He lived with her for about a year; then she threw him over for another man.''

Oh, yes, that sounded like Enid, Mara thought miserably. There had been a string of lovers marching through her aunt's life. She had never been satisfied with any one man for long. Enid had been a totally selfish, heartless woman. It would not have bothered her conscience in the least to seduce a man away from his wife and family, nor to callously toss him out when she'd tired of him. Hers had been a thoroughly hedonistic outlook. The fulfillment of her own desires had been the only thing that mattered to Enid.

A lot of things were becoming clear now. Grant, of course, knew she was Enid's niece, and he'd evidently tarred her with the same brush. It wasn't fair but, in a way, it was understandable. He and his mother had suffered a great deal at Enid's hands. You could hardly expect them to be overjoyed at having her niece for a neighbor.

Suddenly all the pleasure had gone out of the afternoon. Before, there had been a small sense of spiteful enjoyment at having put one over on an arrogant, overbearing, prejudiced man. But not now. It was perfectly natural for him to resent her presence here. In his place, she'd probably feel the same. Mara was consumed suddenly with a horrible sense of guilt and disgust, and shame for what her aunt had done. Edging away from the side of the pool, she started for the ladder at the shallow end. ''I think it's time I went home, Vicky. I really shouldn't have come in the first place.''

''Oh, but . . .''

''I couldn't agree more, Miss Whitcomb.'' Grant's icy words cut across his sister's protest like a well-honed axe.

Both women froze. Mara closed her eyes and held her breath. *Oh God! Now I've done it.*

Vicky's blue eyes grew round with shock as she stared at her brother, looming menacingly at the edge of the pool. "Grant! What are you doing here?"

"Go into the house, Vicky," he ordered, ignoring her question.

Mara could sense Vicky's indecision and turned to place a hand on her arm. "It's all right, Vicky. Go on."

Blue eyes flickering with apprehension, Vicky bit her lower lip. "Are you sure?" Her glance went briefly to Grant, then darted back. "I'll stay if you want me to."

"No, you go on in. This is between your brother and me."

She watched as the younger girl climbed shakily from the pool and scurried across the patio and into the house, aware all the time that Grant's icy gray eyes had never left her. Slowly, Mara turned and faced him, lifting her chin in proud defiance despite her fluttering insides.

He was dressed much as he'd been the first time she'd seen him, only this time his suit was dark blue. He stood with his clenched fists planted on his hips, his coat thrust back to reveal a slender waist and a board-flat abdomen. His legs were braced apart, as though ready to do battle, and the lightweight fabric of his summer suit was stretched taut over long, well-muscled thighs. He looked dangerous.

Mara moved toward the ladder and forced herself to climb out. Water streamed from her body as she stepped onto the surrounding concrete, collecting in an ever-widening puddle around her feet. Her wet, creamy skin glistened in the slanting rays of the setting sun. Mara felt at a distinct disadvantage as she turned and faced Grant's immaculately clad form.

His cold gray eyes slowly inspected her from head to toe. Mara's fingers curled into tight fists as she realized he was having no trouble visualizing her without her bathing suit. Despite the fact that he disliked her, Grant could not control the flash of sexual awareness that flared briefly in his eyes.

"What are you doing here, Miss Whitcomb?" His voice was low, vibrating with tightly leashed anger.

"I was invited. I'm sorry. I realize now that I shouldn't have come."

He walked toward her, and Mara had to fight against an overpowering urge to turn and run. "I thought I'd made myself clear. I don't want you here. I don't want you anywhere near any member of my family."

"Yes. I understand that, and now that I know why, I can promise you it won't happen again."

"What do you mean, 'now that you know why'?" he demanded, zeroing in on the revealing phrase.

She hadn't meant to say that. It had been a slip of the tongue, born of her nervousness and an absurd sense of guilt. But it was out now and there was no way she could take it back. To delay her answer as long as possible, Mara tilted her head to the side and twisted her hair into a rope to wring out the excess water. When done, she tossed the long, wet strands over her shoulder and walked toward the chaise lounge, where her jeans and shirt lay.

"I asked you a question, Miss Whitcomb!"

Mara picked up her yellow print shirt and slipped it on before turning to face him. She looked at him with a calm she didn't feel as her shaking fingers worked the suddenly too-large buttons through their holes. "Vicky told me about my aunt and your father."

His body jerked as though he'd been sprayed with buckshot. He was coldly furious. She could see that. "You've been discussing me with my sister?"

"Not you, Mr. Sloane," she denied quickly. "Your father and my aunt."

A muscle jumping in his jaw warned her of the small explosion that was coming. "Damn!" he swore softly, raking his fingers through his hair. Agitated, he turned away, then swung back immediately, his look accusing. "I didn't want my mother or Vicky to know of your connection with the Price woman. It would only upset them to know."

"She doesn't know. Or at least, if she does, I didn't tell her." Picking up her jeans, Mara briefly considered putting them on, then rejected the idea. Her body was still dripping water and she doubted she could get them on without a lot of undignified pulling and tugging. With a shrug, she draped the jeans over her arm and pushed her feet into her sandals. At least her shirt covered the upper part of her body.

Screwing up her courage, Mara walked over to Grant and stood in front of him, facing him squarely. "I can understand how you feel, Mr. Sloane, and I give you my word, I won't tell Vicky that Enid was my aunt."

When his mouth curled in derisive disbelief Mara drew in a sharp breath. "Don't look at me like that!" she snapped. "I keep my word!"

Stung by the skepticism in his face, she turned sharply and stalked across the patio, heading for the thick stand of trees that marked the beginning of her property. She'd taken no more than a half dozen steps when his hand closed around her upper arm and jerked her to a halt.

"Where do you think you're going?"

His demanding tone brought Mara's head swinging around, and she was surprised to find his face only inches away. His nearness jolted through her like an electric shock. She was acutely conscious of his hard fingers on the soft skin of her arm, the heat from his body flowing around her. The male scent of him assailed her nose, and mingled with it was just the slightest hint of some tangy, masculine cologne and the pungent smell of tobacco. She could even feel the moist warmth of his breath fanning her cheek. Nervously, she pulled back against his hold.

"I'm going home."

"I'll drive you." He turned toward the drive at the side of the house, but Mara hung back.

"No, thank you. I'd rather walk," she replied stiffly. "It's only about a mile, if you take the trail through the woods."

"Nevertheless, I'll drive you home," he insisted. A hateful smile curved his mouth. "It's getting late and we can't have you walking home alone through the woods after dark, now can we?"

Giving her no chance to protest further, his hand tightened its grip and he propelled her forward. Mara practically had to skip to keep up with him. She was beginning to feel distinctly irritated.

"Really, Mr. Sloane. It isn't necessary to use brute force." Her eyes dropped to the hand clasping her arm, then slid back to his face, her expression cool and self-contained. "I'm quite willing to leave, you know."

He stopped and looked at her intently. Mara thought she saw a glint of admiration in those glacial eyes, but it was so fleeting she couldn't be sure. After only a second's hesitation he released her and stepped back, motioning with his hand for her to precede him, but his mouth quirked sarcastically, making a mockery of the polite gesture.

Mustering as much dignity as possible under the circumstances, Mara held her head high and marched down the narrow path toward the sleek, silver-gray Continental parked in the drive. She felt slightly ridiculous, trying to make a grand exit dressed in only a bathing suit and a thin cotton shirt that barely reached her thighs. The hair on the back of her neck prickled with the knowledge that Grant's eyes were trained on her long, bare legs.

At the car he reached around her and opened the passenger door, but when he tried to assist her into the seat Mara resisted. "No, wait." Before he realized her intent, she spread her jeans over the plushly upholstered seat of sky blue velour. "There, that should protect it long enough for me to get home," she murmured, easing herself into the car.

Grant raised his brows at the thoughtful gesture but made no comment.

The drive was made in silence. Mara was feeling stiff and prickly—not exactly angry, but offended nevertheless. She didn't kid herself. His insistence on driving her home was prompted by neither politeness nor consideration. It was painfully clear that she was being shown off the premises. Mara was trying very hard to be understanding, but the man was pushing her patience to the limit.

She turned her head slightly and studied him out of the corner of her eye. His profile had a hard, chiseled clarity that made her fingers itch for a pad and pencil. Her eyes traced the bold angles and planes of his face, admiring the strong, aggressive bone structure and the deeply etched character lines in the sun-bronzed skin. But her appreciation of his rugged, masculine beauty was strictly aesthetic, impersonal. Artistically, he held a great deal of appeal for her. As a man, he barely registered. He was nothing more than a minor annoyance in the background of her life.

When Grant turned into the long, winding drive that led to her house Mara looked away, dismissing him from her mind, and studied the lush, thick woods towering on either side of the narrow lane. Tall, dark green pines dominated the forest, but there were also oaks and wild pecan trees and an occasional elm. It was virgin land, dense and dark, with a thick tangle of undergrowth that made it almost impenetrable. Fleetingly Mara had considered having the brush and brambles cleared away but had decided against it. She liked it as it was; a forest primeval, with only the faint crisscrossing of animal paths allowing access. It had a soothing, healing effect on her. Already, in the few short weeks she had been there, she was beginning to feel better, more at peace. She was still lonely and the incomplete, empty feeling would not go away, but the pain had lessened.

The road opened suddenly into the small clearing, and Grant brought the car to a stop in front of the house. Mara was surprised when he switched off the engine and turned to face her.

"Don't you get lonely here?" he asked, frowning slightly as his eyes wandered over the small open space.

"Lonely?" Mara considered the question for a moment, then shrugged. "Yes, of course I do."

Grant shook his head impatiently. "Then what the hell are you doing here?"

The fiery aureole of red hair framing Mara's face claimed his attention for a moment. Then, very slowly, his eyes lowered, sliding like a caress over the creamy perfection of her skin to inspect each individual feature. Mara could see her image reflected, mirrorlike, in the silvery gray eyes. They glittered with some strong emotion she could not quite decipher, and she wondered what was going on behind that cool, hard mask. "A beautiful woman like you shouldn't hide herself away in the middle of a pine forest."

Mara stared at him, surprised by the harsh intensity in his voice. "What does my physical appearance have to do with it? I'm here because I want to be, and my reasons are my own." Her hand found the door handle and she turned to slide out.

"Why do you stare at me?"

His question stopped her instantly. She turned her head to look at him over her shoulder, her face startled. "What?" The word came out automatically; then, as she realized what he meant, a wry smile curved her mouth. "Oh, that. I'm sorry if I embarrassed you. It's just that I find your face interesting. If things were different between us I'd ask you to pose for me."

Grant slid across the seat, lessening the distance between them. With a feathery touch, he trailed one finger, slowly, sensuously, over the sensitive skin of her inner arm. A shiver ran through Mara as her skin prickled with awareness. Grant leaned closer, his hooded gaze locked on her mouth. "And would I also be invited to see your etchings?" he breathed, as his head moved closer.

Mara stiffened. She assessed him coolly for a moment, then allowed her lips to curve upward in a faint, derisive smile. "If you think you can drive me away with insults, Mr. Sloane, think again."

Dark, angry color ran up under Grant's skin. His face hardening, he moved back across the seat. "Just stay away from my sister, Miss Whitcomb."

Mara climbed from the car and slammed the door. Bending down, she looked at him through the open window. Her green-eyed gaze was clear and direct. "I'm afraid I can't do that. I told Vicky I'd be her friend. And you see, no matter what you think, I *do* keep my word. I won't make any effort to seek her out. I'll promise you that much. But if she comes here, I'll not turn her away."

Grant absorbed that in silence, staring at her intently for a moment, then nodded his head in curt acceptance. "Fair enough." Without another word, he flicked the ignition key, threw the car in gear, and sent it roaring back down the drive.

Mara stood staring after him, shaking her head. *What a strange, intense man.*

Chapter Four

A frown of intense concentration creased Mara's brows as she threaded her car cautiously through the bumper-to-bumper traffic, her body tense and unconsciously braced for a collision at any moment. After the absolute tranquility of the country, the hustle and bustle of Houston was overwhelming.

A pickup swerved dangerously close to the car in front of her and the irate motorist shook his fist. The other man glared back, then zipped ahead as the traffic surged forward. Mara stared in amazement. Had it always been like this? Had she been so accustomed to it she'd simply never noticed? There was a palpable mood of restlessness about the city, an almost suicidal determination to rush. She shook her head in disgust. All this frenetic darting about reminded her of an anthill after someone had stirred it with a stick.

Mara finally brought the car to a halt in the drive of her former home and climbed out, sighing with relief as she started up the walk. Inside the house, Mrs. Mercer was waiting for her. At the sound of the door closing she came bustling into the entry, her face wreathed in smiles.

"Mara, my dear. How nice to see you again. We were so pleased when you called last night to tell us you were coming into town today to use the studio."

Mara set her art box and overnight bag down on the floor and accepted the elderly woman's bony hand. "Thank you, Mrs. Mercer. It's nice to see you too. How are you and Mr. Mercer settling in?"

"Why, very nicely, thank you."

"And do you think you'll like living here?"

The faded blue eyes softened dreamily as they made a slow sweep of the elegant entry hall. "Oh, my dear," she whispered in an awed tone, "who in their right mind wouldn't enjoy living in this lovely home? It's still hard to believe our luck. Imagine being able to rent this place at a price we can afford."

Mara laughed. She would gladly have let them live there for nothing but knew their pride would never allow them to accept that. The Mercers were a retired couple who had been left homeless when their house had burned to the ground a few months before. Mr. Mercer worked part time in the little framing shop where Mara took her paintings, and when she'd heard of their situation she'd offered to let them live in her house for a nominal rent and their services as caretakers. Mara had explained that only occasionally, when working on a portrait commission, would she be using the studio, and even then there would be very few occasions when she would be spending the night. Therefore, she needed someone to live in the house and look after it for her.

It was not strictly true, of course. She could have leased the house for many times the ridiculous rent she was charging the Mercers and still retained the use of the studio. But, as her gaze swept the immaculate interior, Mara was well pleased with her bargain.

"I'm very glad you're happy here. I think this arrangement is going to work out very well for all of us. And
believe me, it takes a great load off my mind, just
knowing you're here."

It was a slight exaggeration, but it was worth it. Mara
was instantly rewarded by the glow of pride in the faded
blue eyes.

Mrs. Mercer patted her hand. "Now don't you worry
about a thing, my dear. We'll take care of this place as
though it were our own." She motioned toward the living
room. "Won't you come in and have a cup of coffee?"

Mara glanced at her watch and shook her head. "I'm
sorry. I really don't have time. Mr. Lowe is due at any
moment for his final sitting." She picked up her bags and
started up the stairs. "When he arrives would you tell him
to come on up?"

"Of course, dear."

Four hours later Mara was standing at the deep utility
sink cleaning her brushes when she heard the sound of feet
clumping heavily up the stairs. She smiled. When the door
opened behind her she didn't even look around.

"Come on in, Chuck. I was beginning to wonder if
you'd forgotten me." Laughter was bubbling in her voice.

"Hi, love. I couldn't believe it when I saw your car in
the drive. Hell! It's been so long since you were here I was
beginning to think you'd forgotten the way. What've you
been doing out in those piney woods? Making eyes at
some moonshiner?"

Mara turned around and grinned. "Of course not! I'm
after the revenuer." She sighed dramatically and rolled
her eyes. "You know how those tough G-men types turn
me on."

Chuck laughed. Then the amusement faded and a look
of deep tenderness and affection warmed his face. She
was looking better, she knew, and could see the knowl-

edge reflected in Chuck's eyes. The violin-string tautness had left her, and slowly but surely, the haunted look was fading.

"Ah, Mara love. It's great to see you again." Chuck surged across the room in three long strides, and before Mara knew it, she was being enveloped in his bearlike embrace. The breath left her lungs in a loud whoosh when he clamped her to his chest and swung her around and around in a wild, exuberant dance. When he finally released her, Mara was gasping for air and her head was whirling. Dazed, she clung to him for support.

"Good grief, Chuck!" she choked, pushing the wildly disordered hair away from her face. "What are you trying to do, kill me?"

"Of course not! Are you crazy?" He gave her a disgusted look that said he was beginning to think she was. "If I did that I'd have to rent my own studio." He grinned suddenly, looking like a naughty little boy. "And I wouldn't have a gorgeous, talented redhead to hang out with anymore. I can't tell you what that does for my ego."

"Huh! Ego, my great aunt! Who do you think you're kidding? The only reason you hang around me is because no one else will listen to all that disgusting mush about your latest ladylove," she scoffed impudently, then blinked in surprise as a strange look flitted across Chuck's face. *What on earth had she said?*

"Yeah, you're probably right." He gave her a rather sickly smile, then immediately changed the subject. "So, what brought you into town?"

"Oh, I had to finish the Lowe commission." Mara waved vaguely toward the portrait on the easel. "And since I had to come into town tonight to attend the Talbots' unveiling party, I decided to kill two birds with one stone."

The abrupt change in mood was confusing her. She and Chuck had always teased one another unmercifully. It was done in jest, as an expression of affection, but they didn't take it seriously. Yet somehow she had struck a nerve.

"Is that party tonight?"

"Don't tell me you forgot! Of course it's tonight. And don't think you're going to weasel out of going. After all, Harry Talbot is *your* boss, and you were the one who persuaded me to do the portrait of their daughter."

Ignoring her outburst, Chuck wandered over to study the finished painting. "You know, love, this is really great," he said in awe. "You certainly have the knack for seeing beneath the facade most people present to the world. It's no wonder your portraits are in such demand. If you wanted, you could spend the rest of your life doing nothing else."

"No, thanks," she replied succinctly. Mara enjoyed portrait work, but her range of artistic interest and ability was too wide to confine herself that way. It was for this reason that she had set a strict limit on the number of portraits she would do each year. As a result, the demand for them had grown, and there was now a long waiting list of people willing to pay an enormous amount for one of her portraits. It was a situation Mara still found a bit puzzling, since her paintings were not really portraits, in the sense that she never painted her subjects formally posed and dressed in their Sunday best. They were really in-depth character studies, rather like being caught in an unguarded moment by a candid photographer.

"So what time are you picking me up for tonight's bash?" Mara asked, refusing to be sidetracked. She wasn't about to go to the Talbots' party alone. She hated that sort of affair. The only reason she'd agreed to go in the first place was for Chuck's sake.

"Well, there's just one little problem." Chuck turned to face her. Ducking his head, he put his hands in his pockets and rocked back on his heels, then looked up sheepishly. "Would it be all right if I brought my fiancée along?"

"Your *what*?"

Mara sat down abruptly on her painting stool and stared at him, her mouth hanging open in astonishment. He was joking! He had to be, she thought dazedly. But as she watched a deep flush spread up over his face all the way to his hairline, she suddenly realized that he was not.

"I know. Shocking, isn't it," Chuck said as she continued to gape at him.

"But when did this happen? How? Who is she? Do I know her?" The questions tumbled out one on top of the other when Mara found her tongue, and Chuck began to laugh and held his hands up for silence.

"Whoa! Whoa! If you'll just calm down, I'll tell you."

Mara looked at him anxiously, eyes wide, and finally he said in a hushed voice, "It's Helen."

"Helen? Helen who?" she demanded, becoming more and more agitated. Then it hit her, and her face grew even more shocked. "Helen! You mean *my* Helen?" The question came out on a rising note that ended in a squeak.

"No," Chuck replied gently. "I mean my Helen."

Mara was stunned. She didn't know whether to laugh or cry. Or both. She couldn't think of any two people in the world who meant more to her than Chuck and Helen, but the idea of them married to each other was mind-boggling. It seemed to her to be a sure prescription for disaster.

She put her hand up and rubbed her forehead distractedly, trying to think. "Chuck . . ."

"I know. It sounds crazy. And believe me, we've been over and over all the logical arguments—we're totally different, we argue all the time. Hell! Helen's even worried because she's a couple of years older than I am. But it's no use. The plain fact of the matter is . . . I love her. And she loves me."

Mara was filled with such a mixture of joy and despair she hardly knew what to say. Chuck was a dear, really. But his emotional attachments had always been so shallow, so fleeting. For all Helen's prickly exterior, Mara knew she was very vulnerable. If this thing between them had already gone as far as an engagement, that meant Helen was head over heels in love and could be hurt very easily. And yet . . . if Chuck really was committed at last . . .

Accurately reading the ambivalent emotions that raced across Mara's face, Chuck reached down and grasped her hands to haul her to her feet. "Look, sweetheart. I know what you're thinking, and I can't really blame you for thinking it, but believe me—this time it's real."

"Oh, Chuck, I hope so." She frowned suddenly and gave him a stern look. "But if you hurt her, so help me I'll never forgive you. And I mean that, Chuck Ainsley!"

"I know that. But there's nothing to worry about. I'm mad about the woman."

Biting her lip, Mara searched his face anxiously. Finally, content with what she saw, Mara relaxed and flung her arms around him. "Oh, Chuck! I *am* happy for you. Honestly I am."

"I know that, love," he whispered, hugging her back. "And I know you're only concerned because you care. That's why we both love you."

Sighing, Mara pulled away from him, looking slightly embarrassed as she wiped the tears from her cheeks. "So, how did this miracle happen? And *when*, for heaven's sake?"

Chuck's face lost that nervous, worried look and he grinned. "Actually, it happened the first night we drove back from your place in the country. We began to realize that with you removed from the scene we wouldn't be seeing much of each other anymore, and suddenly that didn't seem like such a good idea. Of course, neither of us admitted it. But when we got to Helen's she invited me in for coffee and one thing led to another. The next thing I knew, I was kissing her." He sobered then, his face growing tender. "And I can tell you, Mara, nothing, nothing in my whole life has ever felt so wonderful. Or so right."

"I'm glad for you both," Mara said softly, her throat constricting with emotion. She was beginning to feel all choked up and misty again. To keep from bursting into tears she turned and walked over to the sink. Gathering up her brushes, she shaped each one carefully before placing it upright in the drying rack.

"So what's the problem about tonight? I'm sure Helen would love the party. It's just her cup of tea."

"You're right. Except that she has to work late tonight, and I know the Talbots would like you to be there fairly early."

"So? I'll take my car, and you two can come when Helen's through."

"You're sure?"

"Of course. I don't really need an escort. Just moral support."

Mara stood in a corner, sipping ginger ale and trying her best to look inconspicuous. At least, as inconspicuous as someone with flame-red hair could look. She ignored an inviting glance from a tall blond man across the room and peeked at her watch for perhaps the hundredth time. Where on earth were they? Helen and Chuck both knew how she hated these affairs.

Absently, Mara brushed her hand across the skirt of her long gown, needlessly smoothing the clinging fabric over the curve of her hip. It was a deceptively demure dress of white silk crepe, which hung in a straight line to the floor. The knee-high slit at one side allowed her to walk with ease and also provided a tantalizing glimpse of her shapely legs. Long, full sleeves were buttoned tightly at the wrists. The high neckline draped in soft folds across her collarbone, then plunged to her waist in the back, exposing the delectable curve of her spine and a large expanse of flawless skin. She had chosen the dress for its plainness, unaware that against the stark white, her vibrant beauty stood out like a lighthouse beacon on a moonless night.

Catching sight of her reflection in the glass patio door, Mara gave her hair a nervous flick. That night she wore it loose and flowing, pinned back over one ear with a large white silk flower.

The blond man was trying to catch her eye again, and Mara turned her shoulder in a mild but definite rebuff. Lord, how she hated these affairs. Normally, she avoided them like the plague. She had agreed to this one only as a favor to Chuck, and now the idiot wasn't even there!

Still, Mara had to admit she liked the Talbots. They were a pleasant, middle-aged couple who'd been blessed fairly late in life with one child, on whom they doted. Jennifer, far from being the spoiled brat Mara had envisioned, was a charming young girl, and she had quite enjoyed their sessions together. At fourteen, Jennifer was a delightful combination of hoydenish tomboy and budding seductress.

Across the room she saw Helen and Chuck weaving their way toward her. Mara quickly deposited her drink on a convenient table and hurried across to meet them, smiling at the guilty look on Helen's face when she caught her eye.

"And so you should look guilty." Mara laughed and flung her arms around her friend's neck, hugging her tightly. "The very idea, not telling me until now!" She grasped Helen's hands and stood back, beaming. Her radiant smile and sparkling eyes completely belied her scolding words. "I really should give you a good tongue-lashing," she said sternly. "But I'm too happy for you both."

"Oh, Mara. Do you mean it?" Helen's mouth was quivering and her eyes glistened with moisture.

"Oh, no," Chuck groaned. "If you women are going to turn on the waterworks I'm going to need fortification. Point me to the nearest bar."

"Good idea," Mara agreed. "And bring something back for us too. But take your time. I want to talk to this woman."

Chuck threaded his way through the crowd and Helen watched him go with a melting look in her eyes. Seeing it, Mara felt a quick stab of pain slice through her. She could remember looking at David in exactly that way.

When Chuck had disappeared from view Helen slowly turned to face her. Mara was surprised by her wary expression.

"Mara, are you sure you don't mind about Chuck and me?"

"Mind? Why on earth should I mind?"

"Well, I . . . I kind of thought that you and Chuck . . ." She stammered to a halt at the astonished look on Mara's face.

"You're not serious!" Mara squeaked after a moment of stunned silence. "You goose! Chuck and I have been the best of friends for over ten years, but that's all. I love him like a brother. I thought you knew that!"

"Sure?"

"Positive."

Helen's face lit up. "Well, in that case, how would you like to be my matron of honor?"

"I'd love it! When?"

"In three weeks," Helen replied shyly.

Chuck returned with their drinks and they immediately began discussing plans for the wedding. All Mara's apprehensions about Helen and Chuck's alliance dissolved like a wisp of smoke as she watched them together. Helen was bubbling over with joy, and Chuck looked smugly content, like a well-fed cat. He hovered over Helen protectively, adoring her with his eyes, treating her like something too valuable, too precious, to be left unguarded even for a moment. As a result, Helen's face had the soft, luminous glow of a woman who is loved and knows it.

Their happiness was contagious, and Mara found herself relaxing to the point where she was barely aware of the babble of sophisticated party talk floating around them. They had settled the time and place for the ceremony and were discussing the choice of flowers when, out of the blue, Helen suddenly asked, "Tell me, dear. How are you getting along with your hostile neighbor these days?"

Mara shrugged. "I rarely see him. And then only in passing. Why?"

"Because he just walked in, with Vicky and two other women. I'd hazard a guess the older lady is his mother. And since the little blonde is hanging onto his arm like a limpet, I'd say she was his date."

"Oh, no!" A sick dread bubbled up inside Mara. It was bad enough that she had to endure this boring party. To do so under Grant's disapproving eye was just too much!

Chuck's face hardened belligerently. "Don't worry, love. If he makes one nasty crack I'll punch his lights out. In fact, it would give me a great deal of pleasure."

"Chuck, you idiot! You can't do that!" Mara shook her head and gave him a reproving look. "How would it look if you started a brawl at your boss's party? Anyway, I can deal with Grant Sloane."

"Oh, oh. Don't look now, but they're heading this way," Helen whispered.

"Mara! How fantastic! Imagine running into you here, of all places!"

"Hello, Vicky," Mara said, smiling as she met the open astonishment in the younger girl's blue eyes.

Much to Mara's surprise, Vicky had continued to visit, and their friendship had slowly deepened. She was positive Grant was far from pleased, but at least he had left her alone. It had been a little over a month since their encounter by the pool, and during that time, except for catching a glimpse of him occasionally in town, she had not seen him. But now she was uncomfortably aware of him, looming just behind his sister.

"I'll admit I'm as surprised as you are." Reluctantly, Mara let her gaze shift to include the couple who had now moved to Vicky's side, and she felt an immediate tightening of her nerves. Grant was watching her with an icy hostility he made no attempt to hide. His mother had stopped to converse with a group of people on the other side of the room, and Mara wondered if he had deliberately steered her in that direction to avoid this meeting. She could not stem the resentment that flowed through her at the thought. Although she understood his reasoning, it wasn't pleasant being treated like a leper.

Grant gave her a curt nod. "Miss Whitcomb. As you say, this is indeed a surprise." He looked down at the woman hanging onto his arm and smiled. "Janice, this is Mara Whitcomb, our new neighbor. Miss Whitcomb, Miss Janice Holman."

The woman's eyes opened wide in surprise. "Oh! You must be the artist who built that little cabin in the woods." She smiled slowly, her whole attitude one of haughty condescension. "Grant has told me all about you."

Oh, I'll bet he has, Mara thought. I'll just bet he has.

Janice Holman's cool blue eyes were openly assessing, running over her in a way that made Mara want to slap the superior look off her face. Instead, she smiled sweetly, not betraying by so much as a flicker of an eyelash the

irritation she felt. "I'm very pleased to meet you, Miss
Holman. May I present my friends, Helen Thorn and
Chuck Ainsley."

As greetings were being exchanged, a uniformed waiter
glided up bearing a silver tray of brimming champagne
glasses. Everyone except Mara took one. Noticing the
omission, Grant cocked one brow.

"What? Not drinking? Come now, Miss Whitcomb.
We can't have that." He nodded toward the end of the
room, where the Talbot family had gathered around the
sheet-draped easel. "If I'm not mistaken, we're about to
be given a look at this much-vaunted Kendall painting.
You must have a glass of champagne to toast the artist."

His mocking smile and the thin veneer of friendliness
coating his voice made Mara want to scream. This man
was really beginning to annoy her. Why didn't he just take
his snooty little friend and go away? She gave him her
coolest smile. "I'm sorry, Mr. Sloane. I don't drink."

A look of mild surprise crossed Grant's face, but before
he could question her further, Janice Holman broke in.

"Don't you find this terribly exciting? I mean, imagine
actually *owning* a Kendall portrait! My mother would give
her eyeteeth for one." Leaning closer, she whispered
confidingly, "And I understand that the artist is here
tonight, which is most unusual. I don't know about you,
but I'm just dying to meet him." She paused and gave
Mara a narrow look. "But then, since you're an artist,
perhaps you already know him?" The question was asked
in a tone that clearly expressed her doubt of that unlikely
circumstance.

It was a common mistake, but nevertheless Mara's lips
twitched in amusement. She had already achieved a
certain amount of success at the time of her marriage, and
David had insisted that she continue to paint under her
maiden name. Since she signed only the name Kendall to
her work, typically, many people assumed the artist to be

a man. Her identity was not a secret. In fact, it was common knowledge among serious art patrons. But since Mara liked to keep a low profile and actively shunned publicity, very few people outside that circle knew that a Kendall painting was the work of one Mara Kendall Whitcomb.

She was about to clear up the misunderstanding, but the words died on her lips at the sound of Grant's mocking tone.

"Really, Janice. I may not know much about art, but even I have heard of this Kendall fellow. You can hardly expect an artist of his stature to be acquainted with every painter in town."

"Oh, but . . ." Helen's explanation was cut off by a sharp jab in the ribs. Surprise rapidly turned to understanding when she met the hard glitter in Mara's eyes. Only a few people, those who knew her well, could read the portent of that look. The long fuse of Mara's temper had burned down to the end. She had tried to be open-minded and patient, but this man had goaded her once too often. As the Talbots called for quiet, Mara gave him an oblique look. You are about to get your comeuppance, you high-and-mighty, arrogant, pigheaded jerk, she thought gleefully.

Seeing her look, Grant cocked an eyebrow, but Mara merely smiled mysteriously and turned away.

"Ladies and gentlemen, may I have your attention, please."

Chapter Five

Every head turned toward the end of the room. Standing next to the large, satin-draped painting, Harry and Vera Talbot were beaming with pride. Next to them, looking as though she wished she were anywhere but there, Jennifer shifted from one foot to the other and twisted her fingers into knots.

Harry Talbot stepped forward. "Well, my friends. Since you're all aware that you were invited here tonight to witness the unveiling of our daughter's portrait, I won't bore you with a long, unnecessary speech." Turning, he gripped the heavy covering in both hands. "Ladies and gentlemen, our daughter, Jennifer." With one sharp tug, he pulled the slippery satin away from the painting.

The expectant hush was shattered by the murmurs of delight erupting all around the room. Then, as if on cue, a deafening applause broke out, while every head craned to get a better look at the unusual portrait.

Jennifer was depicted poised over the home plate of a baseball diamond, her feet braced apart, a bat gripped tightly in her hands and held back over her right shoulder in readiness. Her face wore a look of intense concentration as she waited for the unseen pitcher to send the baseball hurtling over home plate. Sticking out of the back pocket of her jeans was a pair of pink ballet slippers, their long ribbon ties fluttering out in the breeze. Only after the incongruity of this struck did the viewer notice that the black knit top showing above the waistband of her jeans was actually the top half of a ballet leotard, or that her hair was scraped back and secured in the standard topknot of a ballerina. In the background, leaning against a tree, was her bike. Peeking out over the top of the carryall basket on the front was a frilly pink tutu. The painting clearly stated the emotional tug-of-war that is so much a part of early adolescence. Mara had titled the work "Betwixt and Between."

Finally, when the excitement began to fade, Harry continued with his presentation. "And, as you've all probably heard by now, we're honored to have the artist with us tonight." He stopped and glanced around the room until his searching gaze located the person he sought. Holding out his hand, he said, "Mara, my dear. Would you please join us?"

From the corner of her eye Mara registered Grant's knee-jerk reaction and felt a rush of fierce, righteous pleasure. She could feel his eyes burning into her but resolutely refused even to look his way. Holding her head high, she slipped through the crowd of clapping people and joined the Talbots.

Harry called for silence as he took her hand and turned her toward the crowd. "Ladies and gentlemen, may I present the lovely and talented lady responsible for this beautiful portrait—Mrs. Mara Kendall Whitcomb."

Mara acknowledged the applause with a smile, letting her gaze wander slowly around the room before leveling on Grant. Until that moment she hadn't known that gray eyes could ignite. But his had. They were shooting blue flame.

Later, as she stood in a group that included her host, Chuck, and Helen, Grant and his girl friend approached her. Mara had endured over an hour of well-meaning praise and rather gushing compliments from the Talbots' other guests. She was tired and uncomfortable and in no mood for more of Grant's cutting remarks or Janice Holman's bitchiness.

"Grant. So glad you could make it," Harry said genially as he stepped aside to make room for the pair. "Have you and Miss Holman met our lovely artist?"

"Yes, we have." Grant answered for both of them. "As a matter of fact, Miss—" He paused and smiled sarcastically. "I beg your pardon, I mean *Mrs*. Whitcomb —lives next door to my place in the country." The cold gray eyes impaled Mara. "However, I must admit I didn't make the connection between Mrs. Whitcomb and the Kendall portrait you've been raving about for the last month."

The statement was a direct challenge, and Mara knew it. She returned the hard stare unflinchingly. "Kendall is my maiden name. Since I had already established myself as an artist when I married, my husband insisted I continue to use that name professionally."

"But wouldn't it be more to your advantage to use the name Whitcomb? You're missing out on a lot of publicity, painting under a different name."

"I don't paint for publicity, Mr. Sloane." Mara's voice hardened as she began to see where this line of questioning was leading. He was making his point very subtly, the implied insult going over the heads of the other people present. But Mara didn't miss it. Her avaricious aunt would have used any method at her disposal to drive up the value of her paintings; therefore it followed, at least to

Grant's way of thinking, that she would do the same. The fact that she hadn't, his mocking tone implied, was obviously an oversight on her part.

Fed up to her back teeth with his nasty innuendos, Mara held her head high. Her body was shaking with the rush of unaccustomed fury that consumed her. "I paint because it's what I do best, what I must do," she rasped tightly, her temper very much in evidence. "I'll admit I enjoy the fruits of my labor, but contrary to what you obviously think, I abhor being in the public eye."

"I can attest to that," Harry added with a chuckle. He seemed to be oblivious to the tension that had sprung up between them. "Mara doesn't usually attend affairs of this sort." He clapped Chuck on the back and beamed at him. "But it just so happens that Chuck here, besides being the most talented art director I've ever employed, is also a close personal friend of Mara's. Being the unscrupulous sort of fellow I am, I prevailed upon him to persuade her to come."

The surprise Grant felt at hearing Chuck described in such glowing terms was evident. The two men had been studiously avoiding direct conversation all evening, but now Grant turned to Chuck, his brows drawn down in a puzzled frown. "You're the art director for Talbot Advertising?"

"That's right. Mara and I went to art school together many years ago, but I don't have her talent or dedication, so I turned to the commercial field."

"I see." Grant's attention switched to Helen. "And you, Miss Thorn? Are you an artist also?"

"No, I'm Mara's accountant and general business manager. I take care of the nitty-gritty and leave Mara free to paint."

Janice Holman placed a possessive hand on Grant's arm and edged closer. She stared pointedly at Mara's bare left hand, her eyes narrowed and spiteful. "Tell me, Mrs. Whitcomb, how long have you been divorced?" she inquired silkily.

The question hit Mara like a slap in the face. Then, as the shock began to wear off, she grew rigid with fury. She'd had enough! For the most part she had ignored Grant's insults. He, at least, had some basis for his animosity, unfair and inaccurate though it was. But she was not about to take any guff from his cold-eyed, snotty little girl friend.

"I'm not divorced, Miss Holman. I'm a widow. My husband was killed in a boating accident two years ago." The biting contempt in her voice stated her low opinion of the woman's manners more effectively than a direct insult. A stunned, uncomfortable silence followed and Mara let it hang there.

While the blond woman was still struggling to find her tongue, Mara excused herself to the others and turned to leave. Encountering Grant's stony expression, she lifted her chin, her eyes flaring with the light of battle. If he wanted a knock-down-drag-out fight she was in exactly the right mood to give it to him. Her patience was at an end.

But to her surprise, he merely stepped aside and let her pass. Walking away from the small clutch of silent people, Mara could feel the stab of those gray eyes between her shoulder blades.

Helen found her a few minutes later in the bedroom set aside as a ladies' powder room. Seated on the low bench before the dressing table, Mara was slowly gliding a comb through her fiery hair, going over and over the same tangle-free strands. It crackled and shimmered around the comb like tongues of flame. Mara watched it, her face impassive. She found the steady, rhythmic motion soothing to her frayed nerves.

"Are you all right?" Helen asked worriedly.

Lifting her eyes to Helen's anxious reflection, Mara smiled. "Yes, I'm fine. Don't worry. I'll admit I was very close to losing my temper completely, but I've calmed down now."

"Personally, I don't see how you kept from giving that woman a good smack in the face!" Helen burst out furiously. "That's what I'd have done in your place."

"I was tempted, but sanity prevailed in the end." Mara rooted through her small silver bag until she came up with a coppery lip gloss. With deft movements, she stroked the glistening color over her lips.

Helen leaned forward to inspect her reflection and patted a stray curl back into place. Her eyes lowered to meet Mara's in the mirror. "Are you sure you're going to be all right?"

"Yes, of course. Why do you ask?"

"Because Chuck and I have to leave." She paused and smiled shyly. "We're flying to New Orleans early tomorrow morning so that he can meet my parents. But if you need us, we'll stay," she added quickly.

"Don't be silly. You two go on. I'll be leaving myself just as soon as I say good-bye to Vera and Harry."

"Okay. If you're sure."

Smiling, Mara watched her friend hurry out the door. But the smile faded as she turned back to the mirror, her eyes growing pensive and sad. She was happy for Chuck and Helen. She truly was. Yet their obvious joy in one another seemed to emphasize the barrenness of her own life. Her place in their lives had subtly shifted, which was as it should be. But it brought home to her once again that nothing, nothing in this world, is permanent.

Shaking off the despondent mood, Mara returned the lip gloss to her purse and stood up. With a determined set to her jaw, she squared her shoulders and pushed through the door . . . and came to an abrupt halt.

Propped against the wall, his hands in his pockets, one

foot crossed indolently over the other, stood Grant. He looked completely relaxed and casual, but Mara could sense the coiled-spring alertness behind the lazy facade. And she didn't much care for the look in his eyes. It was suspiciously like that of a cat who has his mouse trapped in a corner and is ready to play.

Mara gave him an arch look and went to step around him, but before she could move Grant's hand snaked out and clamped over her wrist.

"Oh no you don't," he murmured silkily. "You're not going anywhere, *Mrs*. Whitcomb, until we've had a little talk."

Mara gave him a cool, level stare. "I don't believe we have anything to talk about, Mr. Sloane."

"Well, that's where you're wrong." In one fluid motion, he pushed himself away from the wall and turned her around. "We'll talk in here."

"Oh, but . . ."

Before she could complete the protest, Mara was being propelled across the hall and through another door. She heard it click shut behind her as she was thrust unceremoniously into the small room. Momentum sent her staggering forward and she nearly went sprawling across a frilly, organdy-draped bed before she managed to grab the bedpost and right herself. Still holding the post, she whirled around, her eyes glaring.

"I don't know just what the devil you think you're doing, but I'm getting out of here," she insisted in a furious hiss.

Grant smiled complacently. "Oh, really? How?" He was leaning back against the closed door, his arms folded across his chest, the look in his eyes daring her to try.

Mara ground her teeth in frustration. She was no match for him physically, and they both knew it. Haughtily, she tossed the bright fall of hair back over her shoulder. Her face was stiff as she stared back at him, her eyes cold. "All right!" she snapped. "Since I seem to have no choice in the matter, say what you have to say, and let's get it over with."

Grant left the door and walked toward her. "For starters, why the hell didn't you correct me when I called you *Miss* Whitcomb? Why didn't you tell me you were a widow?"

The surprise Mara felt was plain. She had expected him to complain about the setdown she'd given his girl friend and had been mentally marshalling her defenses. This line of attack had very neatly pulled the rug out from under her.

In confusion, she resorted to sarcasm. Sending him a saccharin-sweet smile, she purred, "Why, Mr. Sloane, I wouldn't dream of telling you anything. After all, you claim to know me so well."

His eyes narrowed at the tiny jab, but he continued to stalk slowly toward her. Mara began to feel uneasy. His taunting, casual mask had slipped, and she could see he was furiously angry.

"Why did you let me think you were just another run-of-the-mill artist like your aunt? Did you enjoy making a fool of me? Is that it?"

What he had said about her aunt was true. As an artist, Enid had been merely competent. No more. Technically, her work could not be faulted, but it lacked warmth or any depth of feeling. Enid had never felt love or sorrow, and it had shown.

As Grant's anger increased, Mara grew calm, even somewhat amused. It struck her as slightly ridiculous to be wasting all this emotion on a man who meant absolutely nothing to her. Laughing softly, mockingly, she shook her head. "Mr. Sloane, I didn't make a fool of you. You did that all by yourself. You jumped to conclusions and immediately assumed them to be facts. Before you ever so much as laid eyes on me you set yourself up as judge, jury, and chief prosecutor, and found me guilty.''

He came to a halt directly in front of her, his icy eyes impaling her. ''If I was wrong about you, and I'm still not convinced I was, why didn't you correct me?''

Mara gave him a scathing look. ''Why should I? I don't have to defend myself to you.''

Her cool disdain seemed to infuriate him. His eyes blazed and, as though he could no longer contain his anger, he grasped her shoulders and gave her a hard shake. The white silk flower flew out of Mara's hair and fell to the floor unnoticed. Her loose mane bounced around her shoulders, catching the light like dancing flames. Finally he stopped, hauling her close, his stiff, furious face only inches from hers. ''Don't you even care what other people think of you?'' he demanded.

Mara was stunned by his violent display of temper. What had she done to warrant it? Instinctively, she pulled back against his hold. ''Let me go!''

He gave her another little shake. ''Answer me!''

.''All right! Yes, I care what people think!'' she snapped, then added nastily, ''At least, the people who matter.''

''Meaning I don't, I take it.''

Mara's smile was mocking. ''Right.''

''Damn you,'' he snarled. ''If you don't care, why the hell should I?'' He dragged her closer, and Mara's eyes widened as she read the intent glittering in his eyes.

But it was too late. He bent suddenly and caught her mouth with his. One arm slipped around her back as his other hand thrust upward through her hair, twining the long vivid strands around his fingers to hold her captive. His mouth moved on hers insistently, his probing tongue demanding entrance. Mara struggled against the painful assault, but finally she yielded, unable to stand it any longer, and his tongue plunged deep, deeper, ravaging the sweetness within, devouring and dominating. His hand slid over the bare, smooth skin of her back, forcing her into intimate contact with his hard body, the fingers stroking and kneading a fiery path.

Mara was cold and shivering. Except for Chuck's brotherly bear hugs, no man had touched her in over two years. She couldn't handle this. She felt raw and vulnerable, suffocated by his masculinity and the forced intimacy of his embrace.

Suddenly, as quickly as it had begun, the kiss ended and he thrust her away. Mara swayed on her feet as her knees threatened to buckle beneath her. Pressing a hand to her swollen lips, she stared at him, her face white with shock, her eyes huge. She was breathing hard, her breasts heaving beneath the clinging white gown. "Why did you do that?" she whispered hoarsely.

He looked at her in silence for a moment, then turned away and went to stand by the window. His back was to her but Mara could see the harsh rhythm of his breathing and knew that he, too, was struggling for control. Bending his head, he rubbed the back of his neck wearily. "God knows," he answered finally.

Oddly enough, Mara believed him. Certainly she was the last person he would want to kiss. It had been a spur-of-the-moment thing, born of anger and frustration. It had nothing to do with attraction or desire. He had probably wanted to slap her, but being too much of a gentleman for that, he had resorted to that harsh kiss.

Immensely relieved, Mara sank down onto the edge of the bed.

Grant turned from the window. His face was grim as he walked toward the door. With his hand on the knob, he hesitated a moment, then looked at her. "I'm sorry. I shouldn't have done that." It was a terse apology, given with such obvious reluctance that Mara almost laughed.

"Would you answer a question for me?" she asked quietly when he turned to leave.

Grant tensed. "What?"

"Are you like your father?"

"*No*, damn you! Absolutely not!" He whirled to face her. The heavy black brows were drawn together in a scowl and his jaw was taut. His anger had returned in full force, but she refused to be intimidated. She gave him a look of mild surprise.

"Really? And yet the blood ties between a father and son are much closer than those between . . . say . . . an aunt and niece."

"That doesn't mean that I'm like my—" Grant stopped abruptly, an arrested expression in his eyes. For a tense moment he stared at her, but gradually the rigid anger changed to uncertainty; then, at last, to reluctant acceptance. "I see your point," he conceded finally.

"I hope so. No one likes to be judged on the actions of another, Mr. Sloane. I'm *not* my aunt. I'm Mara Kendall Whitcomb, a totally separate individual." She spoke with a quiet, determined dignity that Grant seemed to find fascinating. His eyes burrowed into her and Mara met the searching look with unflinching directness. "I'm truly sorry my aunt caused you and your mother so much unhappiness and pain. But I'm not responsible for her actions, and I refuse to be persecuted for them."

He hesitated for a second. Then, his mouth compressed in a grim line, he gave her a curt nod and left without another word.

With a sigh, Mara walked to the small dressing table in the corner and checked her appearance. After running a comb through her hair and reapplying her lip gloss she turned and started toward the door. The white silk flower lay on the floor, forgotten.

Ten minutes later, when she turned out of the Talbots'

long drive onto the quiet residential street, Mara had dismissed Grant Sloane from her mind.

It was very late. The dimly lit streets were all but deserted. A sudden drowsiness produced a prodigious yawn, and Mara hastily rolled her window down partway. She shivered and snuggled deeper into her coat. Somehow she had to stay alert.

The lights of the freeway were only about two blocks ahead when, without warning, the engine suddenly coughed and died. Bewildered, Mara turned the steering wheel and allowed the car to coast in as close to the curb as she could get before the wheels stopped turning. As she switched off the ignition, her eyes swept the deserted street for some sign of help. There was none, not even a telephone booth. With a sigh, Mara pulled out the emergency signal button and settled down to wait. Sooner or later someone had to come along. She didn't even consider looking under the hood. The inner workings of a car engine were a complete mystery to her.

She had waited a bare five minutes when the lights of another vehicle pierced the back window of her car. Mara straightened and turned eagerly to greet her would-be rescuer, but her hopeful expression dissolved when the powerful motorcycle roared to a stop beside her door. The dim light from the streetlamp revealed the leering expressions of its two scruffy riders as they gave Mara and her car a quick once-over. They were both young, no more than eighteen or nineteen; yet, despite their youth, there was an unnerving aura of menace about them. When the one riding pillion dismounted and started toward her with a lazy, indolent swagger, Mara's heart began to thump painfully.

"Well, hello, doll," he drawled insolently, bracing his hands on the side of the car and ducking down to peer at her through the open window. The leering grin widened as his eyes roamed over her. "Looks like you've got yourself some serious trouble, gorgeous."

Mara's stomach contracted in a spasm of sickening fear. From the look in his eyes she knew he wasn't referring to her stalled car. Swallowing hard, she fought a silent battle with her fluttering nerves.

"Uh . . . as you can see, my car won't run. Would you mind phoning a tow service for me?" she asked. It was pure bluff, and they both knew it, but she refused to let him see just how much he frightened her.

The youth threw his head back and laughed aloud. The harsh, mirthless sound bounced through the empty street. "Nice try, lady." He chuckled. "But I'm afraid the only help you're gonna get tonight will be from me'n my buddy."

Mara jumped and tried to evade his hand as it snaked into the car, but before she could move out of range he had grabbed a hand full of her hair and twisted it around his wrist.

Panic-stricken, Mara lashed out blindly with both hands, raining ineffectual blows about his face and head. He laughed cruelly until her bunched fist made sharp contact with the tender flesh of his nose. A low grunt was quickly followed by a vicious yank on her hair. Mara gasped as fiery needles of pain seared across her scalp and tears sprang into her eyes.

He brought his face close to hers, his lips drawn back over yellowed teeth in an ugly snarl. His fetid breath made Mara's stomach churn. "Now, why don't you be a good girl and climb out peaceably," he grated in a low, menacing tone. "It'll be a tight squeeze, but I think we can ride three on the bike."

Mara was so terrified she didn't notice the lights of the other car until it squealed to a stop behind her own.

The young man beside the car turned to glare at the intruder, but his friend on the bike wasn't quite so brave.

"For Chrissake, Al! Let's get the hell out of here!" he yelled, revving up the bike's powerful engine.

Mara's young assailant hesitated for a second, but the slamming of a car door seemed to galvanize him into action. Quickly he released her hair, whirled around, and jumped astride the already moving bike.

Faint with relief, Mara slumped forward over the steering wheel. Over the rapidly receding roar of the motorcycle engine she was vaguely aware of the sound of running feet pounding toward her, but she was too shaken to move.

"Mara! Mara, for God's sake! Are you hurt?" Before she could answer her door was jerked open. Someone gripped her shoulders and pulled her upright. Masculine hands pushed the shimmering waves of hair away from her face, and their very gentleness gave Mara the courage to open her eyes.

"Grant?" The name was whispered in dazed surprise as she found herself looking into a pair of glittering gray eyes. He was hovering over her, his brows drawn together. She stared at him, unable to believe for a moment that he was real.

"Did they hurt you, Mara?"

"Oh, Grant!"

Her eyes flooded with helpless tears and she reached out for him in frantic desperation, reacting instinctively to the urgent note of concern in his voice.

After only the barest hesitation, Grant slipped his arms around her and hauled her from the car. He cradled her against his chest, rocking her back and forth gently as he murmured in her ear. "You're okay now, Mara. No one's going to hurt you. You're safe."

She clung to him, trembling uncontrollably, and burrowed her head against his chest. Long, racking sobs shook her to her toes. Grant merely held her close and let her cry it out. Mara had no idea how long they remained that way, but finally she became aware of the soothing drone of his voice and the steady beat of his heart beneath her ear. Breathing deeply, striving for control, Mara pressed her palms against his chest and took a half step backward. It was only then that she realized they were standing in the glare of his car's headlights, in full view of its three occupants. Giving him a wavering smile, she took another step backward and his arms fell away.

"Th—thank you." She reached up and raked shaking fingers through her hair, massaging her tender scalp. "If you hadn't come along I . . ." The words choked off as her voice began to break with remembered fear.

"Don't think about it," he commanded gruffly. "It's over."

Grant reached inside her car and retrieved her purse and keys, then rolled up the window and locked the door. Cupping her elbow, he urged her toward the silver Continental.

The next thing Mara knew she was sitting in his car, squeezed between him and a very hostile Janice Holman.

Grant placed his arm along the seat behind her head and looked back over his shoulder. "Reach under the seat, Vicky, and get the flask of brandy out of the first-aid kit."

There was a rustle of movement behind them. In the next instant Grant was holding the flask to Mara's lips. She jerked her head back; the fumes nearly took her breath away.

"No. I don't want it," she protested. "I told you, I don't drink."

"This is strictly for medicinal purposes. You've had a shock, and you need it. Now drink." Mara looked at him wide-eyed. The implacable expression on his face left her in no doubt that he would pour the fiery liquid down her throat if she didn't obey him. Reluctantly she put a shaking hand over his and tipped up the flask to take a tentative sip, then made a face. It was vile! She tried to push it away, but Grant wouldn't let her.

"Come on. Drink some more," he urged softly.

"Oh, for heaven's sake!" Janice snapped. "Leave her alone if she doesn't want it. She looks perfectly fine to me anyway."

"Shut up, Janice."

The startled woman opened her mouth to object but a quelling look from Grant stopped her, and she flounced back in her seat, fuming silently.

At his insistence, Mara took several more sips of brandy. Vaguely, she wondered why she was letting him take charge of her this way. Her throat felt as though it had been cauterized by liquid fire!

"Is she all right, son?" Mrs. Ridgeway's pleasant, well-modulated voice was laced with concern.

"Yes, Mother. I think so." Grant screwed the cap back on the flask, and Mara leaned her head back against the seat and closed her eyes. "All she needs now is rest and a chance to recover."

Mara didn't like the way they were discussing her as though she weren't there. She wanted to protest but was just too exhausted. The brandy was already taking effect, its warmth bubbling through her veins and making her drowsy.

She felt a gentle hand touch her hair. "Mara? Are you sure you're all right?" Vicky's voice quivered with uncertainty and fear, and Mara felt a little warmer. At least she had one friend in this car.

"Yes, Vicky. I'm fine now."

"Wake up, Mara."

The voice came from a long way off, and Mara stirred restlessly. A hand shaking her shoulder broke through the sleepy haze and she blinked, then opened her eyes

completely, frowning as she tried to identify her surroundings.

"You're home now, Mara. Wake up."

Grant's deep, rumbling voice, coming from somewhere
just above her head, brought her awake in a flash. Mara sat
bolt upright, flushing hotly as she realized she'd been
sleeping with her head on his shoulder. For a confused
moment she couldn't imagine what she was doing in a car
with him, of all people. Then memory came rushing back,
and she shivered.

"Are you okay?"

"What? Oh! Yes, I'm fine, just a little cold," she lied.
She picked up her purse and scooted across the seat.
Twisting around, she opened her mouth to say goodnight
to Vicky and Mrs. Ridgeway and found herself staring
into an empty back seat. Mara looked at Grant in
confusion. "Where are the others?"

"I took them home before bringing you here." She
thought he smiled, but with only the soft glow from the
dash to light up the interior of the car it was difficult to
tell. "Mother wanted you to stay with us tonight, but I
assured her you'd be more comfortable in your own
home."

Mara had to battle down the urge to laugh. She could
imagine his reaction to that suggestion! She gave him a
wry smile. "Yes, of course."

"I'll call my garage and have your car towed in," he
informed her as she reached for the door handle. "When
it's repaired I'll take you into town to pick it up."

Leave it to a man to be practical, Mara thought. She had
completely forgotten about the car. When Grant had
arrived on the scene she'd been so relieved she'd walked
away without giving it another thought. Mara bit her
bottom lip worriedly. She really didn't want to accept any
more favors from this man, yet she had to admit it was the
most sensible solution.

"Thank you. I appreciate that." Mara paused, then added softly, "And thank you very much for coming to my aid tonight. I don't know what I'd have done if you hadn't."

Surprising her, he reached out and touched her face, running his fingertips slowly down the elegant line of her cheek and jaw. "Try not to think about it," he whispered huskily. His eyes slid past her to the darkened house, then came back to rest on her face. She couldn't be sure, but she thought there was a glimmer of genuine concern in the gray depths. "Will you be all right here alone?" After a brief hesitation he added, "If not, you're welcome to come back with me."

"No, thank you. I'm used to being alone." Mara turned and opened the door. "Goodnight, Grant."

"Goodnight, Mara."

He remained where he was until she had unlocked the door and stepped inside. As she flipped on the living-room lights the low purr of the powerful engine receded down the drive, then faded away.

Mara felt a sudden chill and shivered. Frowning, she tossed her coat and purse onto the sofa and paced back and forth in front of the fireplace, rubbing her forearms briskly. This was silly! Why now, after all these weeks of living here, did she suddenly feel so lonely? Why did the house seem so quiet, so empty?

With an impatient sigh, Mara gathered up her things and marched into the bedroom. She was just suffering from a bad case of nerves, and delayed reaction to that frightening incident earlier. All she needed now was a good night's rest. By tomorrow everything would be back to normal.

Chapter Six

The sky was aflame. Streaks of hot pink, gold, purple, and fiery orange blazed in the deepening, dusky blue. Against the brilliant backdrop, tall pines looked almost black, their feathery edges gilded a glowing yellow. A willow stood forlornly by the small pond and trailed its graceful, drooping branches in the shallows next to the bank. The water was calm, glass-smooth, its mirrorlike surface shimmering with the vibrant colors of the setting sun and throwing back an exact image of the willow.

Mara added another stroke of the rosy gold color, then stepped back and cocked her head to one side.

"Very nice."

The deep, drawling voice came as a complete surprise, and she jumped with fright. Whirling around, Mara clutched her brush and palette to her like a shield, then slumped with relief when she spied Grant lounging casually against the railing at the top of the stairs.

"You scared the wits out of me," she breathed in a shaken voice.

"I *did* knock. But I guess you were so engrossed you didn't hear me." He crossed his arms over his chest and lowered his head, looking at her from under his bushy black brows like a stern parent. "Didn't anyone ever tell you to keep your doors locked?"

"Why? The house isn't even visible from the highway. Surely we don't have to worry about crime this far out in the country."

"My God, woman! Didn't that little episode the other night teach you anything? You're defenseless here, all alone. Anyone could walk in."

Mara's eyes widened at the vehemence of his tone, but she thought it wise not to pursue the subject. She placed her palette on the work table and picked up a rag to wipe the excess paint off her brush. "Did you drop by just to scold me, or was there something you wanted?"

"Have you forgotten we're supposed to drive into Houston today to pick up your car?"

"Oh! I'm sorry. I'm afraid I got to painting and forgot all about it." Hastily, she stuck the brushes into a jar of turpentine. "If you'll give me fifteen minutes to scrub off the paint, I'll be ready," she called over her shoulder, racing for the stairs.

After a hasty shower, Mara dressed in a brown corduroy skirt and a cream turtleneck sweater and pulled on a pair of brown suede boots. A quick glance at the bedside clock sent her scurrying to the dressing table. She applied just a touch of moss green shadow to her eyelids and stroked on coppery lip gloss. After dragging a brush through her hair, she slipped several gold chains around her neck, then snatched up her purse and headed for the door.

Grant was roaming around the living room, eyeing it with interest. He looked up at her entrance and gave her a half smile. "Dead on time. You're an unusual woman."

Mara took her coat from the entry closet, then waited

expectantly, but Grant seemed in no hurry to leave. "This is a lovely place," he complimented, his gaze running thoughtfully around the large room. "You have very good taste."

"Thank you," Mara replied dryly. She could see he had not expected that. He was still having trouble reconciling the image he had created of her in his mind with the real woman.

Grant wandered over to the bookcase and picked up the small, silver-framed photograph. He stared at it for so long she began to wonder what he was thinking. She could read nothing in his face. It was as though he had deliberately schooled his features into a bland mask to disguise his inner feelings. There wasn't a trace of the hostile man she had come to expect. He was withdrawn, almost a stranger. He was dressed in slim-fitting black trousers and a black, rolled-neck sweater. Over it he wore a smoky gray suede jacket. To Mara, the casual elegance of his attire seemed to emphasize his air of remoteness.

He continued to stare at the photograph for several minutes. Finally he returned it to the shelf and slanted Mara a brooding look.

"Your husband?"

"Yes."

His gaze swung back to the photo. "Nice-looking guy."

Mara remained silent. David had been so much more to her than just an attractive man. He had been her friend, her lover, her soul mate. But she wasn't going to try to explain that to Grant Sloane. He probably wouldn't believe her anyway.

"Was he an artist also?" he asked quietly.

"David?" She laughed. "No. He was an attorney. He couldn't draw a straight line and had trouble telling a Renoir from a Picasso, but he was absolutely brilliant in a courtroom," she said with quiet pride, her face softening as her gaze went to the photograph.

Grant watched her closely, his expression shuttered. "Did you love him?"

She gave him a startled look. "What a question! Of course I loved him. I married him."

"People do marry for other reasons."

"Well, I don't," she snapped, irritated by the calm, matter-of-fact statement. What was he accusing her of now? Marrying for money? Mara swung her coat over her shoulders and turned toward the door. "Shall we go?"

Grant followed without a word.

Trivial conversation was impossible between them. During the drive Mara kept her gaze trained on the passing scenery. The hum of the tires on the pavement was the only sound in the oppressive silence. How, she wondered, as she watched the forest whizzing by, had they gotten caught up in this crazy situation? It was an ironic twist of fate, to say the least, that Grant had been the one to come to her rescue. Having done so, he probably felt obligated to help retrieve her car. She was sure he had no more desire for her company than she had for his.

"My mother was too embarrassed to introduce herself to you at the party the other night," Grant said, breaking the lengthy silence. "She feels she's been discourteous in not paying you a neighborly visit before now."

Mara sent him a sharp glance, suspecting sarcasm, but his face was still set in the same impassive mask. She returned her gaze to the road. "She needn't," she assured him flatly. "I've a fair idea why she's stayed away."

"I don't deny it was at my insistence," Grant admitted with blunt honesty. "But after seeing you the other night and listening to Vicky's glowing praise, she's decided I was mistaken in my assessment of you." He took his eyes off the road long enough to give her a crooked smile. "As you can imagine, I'm well and truly in the doghouse with the women in my family.''

Mara didn't reply to that. Surely he didn't expect sympathy from her?

"Of course, if you were willing, you could help me get back in their good graces," he said casually, and Mara's head swung around, her expression wary.

"Oh? And just how could I do that?" And why on earth should I? she added silently.

"Are you still interested in painting Vicky?"

"Of course."

"It occurred to me that if I commissioned you to paint Vicky's portrait it would appease both Mother and Vicky."

Mara couldn't believe what she was hearing. He was actually going to allow her near his precious family? She cocked her head to one side. "Does this mean you've changed your mind about me? That you're no longer afraid I'll contaminate your sister?"

"Let's just say I've decided to reserve judgement, shall we?"

Mara's mouth tightened and she returned her gaze to the road. What else had she expected? To be welcomed with open arms? Since the night of the party, Grant's attitude toward her had thawed somewhat, but by no stretch of the imagination could it be described as friendly. By silent mutual consent they seemed to have reached some sort of truce, but it was definitely an armed truce, and Mara knew she'd do well to remember that.

"Very well," she said after a prolonged silence. "I'll paint Vicky on one condition."

"Which is?"

"That I be allowed to use her portrait in my next showing."

He shrugged. "If Mother and Vicky have no objections, that's fine with me."

To Mara's astonishment, when they reached the garage Grant checked her car over thoroughly and questioned the mechanic in detail regarding the repairs. When he was satisfied, she paid the bill, and he walked her to the car.

"Thank you very much for all your help. I . . ."

"Never mind that. I'm going to follow you home."

"Oh, but that's not necessary," Mara protested. "Anyway, I have to stop by my studio to pick up some things."

"So? You don't plan on staying long, do you?"

"No, but—"

"Look," Grant interrupted impatiently. "It'll be dark in another half hour, and I don't want you driving home alone. I'm going to follow you."

Mara stared at him in astonishment. It was a statement, not a request, and she knew nothing she could say would change his mind.

"Oh, all right." Fuming, she slid in behind the wheel.

Twilight was rapidly fading when she stopped the car in the drive of her Houston home. The soft glow of light spilling from the house looked warm and welcoming. There was a sharp nip in the air that meant frost by morning.

Grant parked behind her and was there to open her door before she could step out. When she turned toward the house his hand settled lightly on the back of her waist to guide her up the walk. Mara wanted to step forward and shrug off his touch but, aware that it was merely a polite gesture, she forced herself to ignore it.

Since she hadn't called to give the Mercers warning of her arrival, she rang the doorbell instead of letting herself in. Mrs. Mercer's faded blue eyes lit up in pleased surprise when she opened the door.

"Why, Mara dear. How nice to see you! Whyever did you ring the bell? Did you forget your key?" Smiling, she opened the door wide and motioned them inside.

"No. I just didn't want to barge in on you." Mara

caught the curious glances Grant was receiving and smiled. "Mrs. Mercer, may I present Mr. Grant Sloane."

"How do you do, young man."

Grant took the bony hand she extended and smiled gently. "I'm very pleased to meet you, Mrs. Mercer."

"Mr. Sloane is my neighbor in Montgomery," Mara explained quickly, not caring for the speculative look in Mrs. Mercer's eyes. "He was nice enough to drive me into town to pick up my car at the garage, and I thought, since I was here, I'd get a few things I need from the studio."

"Of course, my dear. Heavens! You know you're welcome anytime. Why don't you just go on up and collect whatever it is you want while I take your young man in to meet Mr. Mercer?" She smiled at them serenely, her face wearing a soft, dreamy look.

"Oh, but you don't understand. Mr. Sloane is just—"

"Go on, Mara," Grant interrupted. "I'll be perfectly happy to wait for you here."

Mara couldn't believe her eyes when she looked at him. She had expected Grant to be angry, but he was actually enjoying this! She stared openly at his wicked smile and the tiny laugh lines that crinkled attractively around his eyes. It was the first time she had ever seen him smile naturally, and it did amazing things to that stern, harshly male face. Briefly, she caught a glimpse of the charm both Helen and his sister had assured her he possessed in abundance.

He looked up and caught her staring, and she could see the shutters come down over his eyes as the mask slipped back into place. Giving her a curt nod, Grant cupped his hand under Mrs. Mercer's elbow to escort her into the living room.

Bemused, Mara turned and climbed the stairs. He really did have the most interesting face. She wondered if she dared ask him to pose.

Mara quickly gathered blank canvases and extra tubes of paint from the storeroom and stacked them at the top of the stairs. In the studio, she began to riffle through the stack of sketch pads piled on the work table, looking for a particular scene she had sketched in France the previous spring. She had been meaning to paint it ever since her return, but somehow, during the move to the country, it had been misplaced in the shuffle. She had been searching for perhaps twenty minutes when Grant appeared in the doorway.

"Can I help you with something?" he asked.

Mara gave him a vague smile and continued to flip through the pages. "No, I don't think so, thank you. I'm looking for a particular sketch." When she reached the last page in the pad she sighed and tossed it aside, then picked up the next one on the stack. "It has to be in one of these." Frowning, she paused to look at him. "But if you're in a hurry, please don't let me keep you."

"No hurry." Grant slid his hands into his pockets and began to stroll around the large, open room. His expression thoughtful, he studied not only the paintings lining the walls and stacked in the corners but the studio itself. "Is this the only room up here?" he asked in a casual tone.

"Yes. Except for the storeroom," she replied distractedly and picked up another pad.

"No bedrooms?"

The odd note in his voice caught Mara's attention, and she glanced up, her expression puzzled. "No. Why do you ask?"

Grant turned and stared at her; then one side of his mouth quirked upward. "It seems I owe you an apology."

"Oh?" One delicate brow rose in question. Privately, she thought he owed her about a half dozen apologies.

"That first time I came here, when Ainsley appeared on the stairs looking so disheveled? I assumed the two of you had been up here in bed together. Obviously I was wrong.''

Mara's face flamed. She lowered her gaze to the pad in her lap and resumed her search. Page after page went flipping past her eyes but she didn't see one of them. She was shaking with resentment. It was a tight, burning knot in her chest.

Grant shifted his feet and jingled the change in his pocket restlessly. He waited for her to speak, but she remained stubbornly silent. ''Well, what the hell was I supposed to think?'' he burst out, shooting her a strange, resentful look. ''You opened the door wearing that slinky green thing. It was obvious that you had nothing on beneath it.''

Mara was startled. Had she? The events of that morning were rather muddled in her mind. The only clear recollection she had was of the overwhelming hostility this man had radiated and the nasty insults he'd hurled at her. Reluctantly, she conceded that, from a stranger's point of view, the situation could have easily been misinterpreted. She cast him a sidelong glance from under her lashes, her green eyes still smoldering.

''Chuck was up here painting. He uses the studio now and then.'' Her voice was cool and clipped, her face stony. It wasn't much of an explanation, but it was all she intended to give him. Mara was still furious, though why, she didn't know. She'd known all along that Grant had a low opinion of her. Keeping her head down, she resolutely refused to look at him.

Several seconds ticked by. The only sound to break the thick silence was the soft flutter of turning pages.

''Are you going to accept my apology, Mara?'' Grant finally asked.

That tersely worded statement was an apology? A bitter laugh rose in her throat. With a determined effort, Mara managed to force it down. It would have given her a great deal of pleasure to throw his damned apology back in his face, but she didn't. For over five months Grant had been popping up in her life, and every encounter had been fraught with bitterness and anger. The emotional turmoil was unsettling. She wanted an end to it. And she accepted that for a man as proud as Grant, even that much of an apology had been difficult. Sighing, Mara lifted her gaze to his.

"All right," she agreed grudgingly. "Considering the circumstances, I suppose I can see where you might have gotten the wrong impression. Let's just forget it, shall we?"

The strange, indecipherable look in his eyes as he stared back at her sent a tiny frisson of alarm up Mara's spine. But finally Grant nodded his agreement, and Mara dismissed it from her mind, returning her attention to the pad in her lap.

Grant strolled over and sat down on the edge of the table. His leg brushed hers, and without conscious thought Mara shifted so that their bodies no longer touched. He shot her a hard glance, his mouth firming as he took in her bent head, her total absorption in her task.

"I've just had a most enlightening conversation with the Mercers," he said to the top of the shining fall of hair. "They were most anxious to tell me all about their beautiful and generous benefactor."

"Ummmm. The Mercers are very nice people," Mara replied absently, not really hearing him. She stopped to study a drawing of a French country cottage. Holding it out at arm's length, she cocked her head to one side, a small frown creasing her brow. The action sent a curling tendril of hair tumbling across her cheek. She went to push it back but Grant's hand was there first, his fingertips feathering softly over her silken skin as he smoothed the shining lock away from her face. The oddly caressing touch acted on Mara like a live wire, and she jerked back, her eyes wide and startled.

"This whole thing is a little impractical, isn't it?" Grant asked, holding her gaze.

He had her attention now, but Mara hadn't the least idea of what he was talking about. She stared up at him, bewildered. "Impractical?" She shook her head. "I don't understand."

"I'm talking about the arrangement you have with the Mercers. Surely you realize you could get many times what you're charging them in rent?"

"They told you what they pay in rent?" Mara's face was blank with astonishment.

"Yes." Grant smiled slowly, his eyes glinting with a strange look. "They were most anxious to impress upon me what a wonderful and generous person you are."

"That's ridiculous! It's an arrangement that suits both sides." Agitated, Mara stood up and began to gather together the pads that littered the table. She would just take them with her and continue her search at home.

"And what does your astute business manager think of this lopsided arrangement? Somehow I don't think the oh-so-efficient Ms. Thorn would be pleased."

Remembering Helen's reaction, Mara grimaced. "You're right. I thought she was going to have apoplexy."

"So . . . you know you could get a mint for this place, yet you prefer to rent it to an elderly couple for next to nothing." Grant looked at her narrowly, searching her embarrassed face. "Why?" The question was asked with a soft determination that made Mara's skin prickle.

"Why not?" she countered nonchalantly. "I don't need the money."

His eyes narrowed even further. "Why should you assume financial responsibility for a couple who are not even related to you?"

The relentless probing was beginning to fray her nerves. Mara didn't care much for the hard gleam in his eye or the suspicious note she thought she could detect in his voice. Slamming down the stack of sketch pads, Mara whirled to face him, both hands planted on her hips. She eyed him coldly.

"Look, Mr. Sloane. It's *my* house, *my* money, and *my* decision," she stated slowly and precisely, each word coated with ice. "If I want to allow an elderly couple to live here for practically nothing, that's my business. I'm fed up with your constant suspicions and insinuations. Is it so impossible to believe that I have no ulterior motive? That I just wanted to help them?" When he opened his mouth to speak she waved aside his comment, shaking her head in weary resignation. "Okay, so you have a low opinion of me. Fine. I've accepted that. And quite frankly, Mr. Sloane, I don't give a damn. But don't you think it's time you stopped belaboring the point?" she asked with aloof, quiet dignity. "I got the message quite some time ago."

Grant's face was an impenetrable mask. Mara had no idea whether he was angry, amused, or just indifferent. "I don't suppose it would occur to you that I was merely trying to get to know you better, to understand what makes you tick?"

"No, you're right. It wouldn't. There would be no point to it. You and I can never hope to be friends. If we both work at it very hard we just *may* be able to achieve a peaceful coexistence, but anything else would be an exercise in futility."

Grant stood up and came around the table to pick up the

heavy stack of sketch pads. "Maybe you're right," he conceded. "Friendship is not what I want from you."

On the drive home Mara couldn't dismiss Grant's words from her mind. On the surface his attitude seemed fairly straightforward; he was prepared to tolerate her for the sake of his mother and sister, but he didn't like her. Yet she couldn't shake off the feeling that there had been another meaning behind his pronouncement.

Mara flicked a quick glance at the rearview mirror and frowned. The headlights reflected there were a constant reminder that her self-appointed bodyguard was still on her trail. It made her feel strange to have him hovering over her like this. He acted as though it was his right to look after her, and his autocratic attitude got under her skin.

And yet, perversely, some deep-seated feminine instinct delighted in his male dominance. It made her feel warm and cherished. It was a feeling she hadn't experienced since David's death. Mara tried to squash it, but it was no use. Her very soul cried for . . . what? Something. Something she could not quite pin down. Human warmth, maybe? A tender touch? Some small sign that she was not completely alone, something that would ease the aching void that had been a part of her for so long? Independence was all well and good, but everyone needed to know there was someone who cared.

Mara gave a soft, bitter laugh as the absurdity of that thought struck her. Grant didn't care whether she lived or died. Why on earth was she going all warm and fluttery just because the man was following her home?

Her eyes flicked again to the mirror. Why was he doing it? According to Vicky, Grant was extremely considerate and protective of the women in his family, but that didn't explain his solicitous behavior toward her. He didn't like or trust her, so why should he insist on protecting her this way?

Tired of wrestling with the insoluble puzzle, Mara released a resigned sigh as she flicked up the turn indicator and swung the car into the narrow drive leading to her home. It was probably just some lingering code of the West; women were weak, fragile creatures who needed to be protected. Grant might despise her, but he felt honor bound to provide that protection when he was in a position to do so.

When Grant had seen her to the entrance of her property, Mara expected him to continue on to his own home, but to her surprise he turned into the lane directly behind her. For heaven's sake! This was carrying duty a bit far! The long, winding drive through the woods somehow seemed even longer with his headlights winking in her mirror. There was a grim set to her lips when she stopped the car in front of the house and climbed out. She waited for Grant while he parked behind her and stepped from the car.

"I appreciate your escort home," she began as he approached. "But it really wasn't necessary for you to follow me all the way to the house."

"I told you I'd follow you home, and I meant it," he informed her, taking her arm as they climbed the porch steps to the front door. He took the key from her hand and unlocked the door, then reached inside and flicked on the light switch.

Mara stepped inside and turned, her hand outstretched for the key. "Good night, Grant. And thank you very much," she said in polite dismissal. She waited expectantly for him to hand her the key and leave, but he merely stared at her, his gray eyes boring into her.

Without warning, Grant took her by the waist and lifted her out of the way, ignoring her shocked gasp of protest.

"What do you think you're doing?" she demanded angrily, clutching at his shoulders.

Grant put her down and swept his eyes around the large, open room, then moved with purposeful steps toward her bedroom. Mara watched in open-mouthed amazement as he made a methodical search of the remaining downstairs rooms, then took the stairs to the studio two at a time. At the top he paused and, after a quick visual search, turned and came down again.

Mara met him at the bottom of the steps, her expression indignant "I asked you a question, Grant. Just what do you think you're doing?"

"I'm making sure there are no intruders," he said quietly. His face was very serious, and he looked down at her with a light in his gray eyes that took her by surprise. "This may be a sleepy rural area, Mara, but we have our share of undesirables too. It doesn't take long for word to get out, and by now I'm sure everyone knows you live here all alone." Concern deepened the frown line between his brows as his eyes roamed over her face. "You're a very beautiful woman, Mara." His voice was deepening, warming to a husky pitch that unnerved her. "You shouldn't be living here all alone. You need someone to look after you, to care for you and keep you safe."

His words echoed the desperate yearnings that had plagued her thoughts all the way home. Mara felt the familiar ache return full force. Unable to meet his serious, intent stare, she turned away. She shrugged off her coat and walked across the room to drop it in a chair. She crossed her arms and hugged herself tightly. "I appreciate your concern, but I'm afraid it's rather wasted on me," she said over her shoulder, keeping her back to him. "Except for the five years of my marriage, I've always been alone. It's certainly no new experience."

Grant's dark brows drew together in a puzzled frown. "What the hell is that supposed to mean?"

"Nothing, really," Mara said quickly, afraid she'd revealed more than she had intended. "I was just trying to explain that I really don't need protection. I'm quite accustomed to taking care of myself."

"Like you took care of yourself the other night, I suppose?" he snapped angrily. "Do you have any idea what would have happened to you if I hadn't come along when I did? What does it take to make you understand that it isn't safe for any woman to be on her own, especially one as beautiful and desirable as you?"

His concern for her well-being seemed out of character, and Mara searched her mind for a logical explanation for it. When one occurred, she turned, her eyes narrowed suspiciously. "What is this, Grant? Another attempt to drive me away? Do you think if you frighten me enough I'll return to the city and get out of your hair? Well, I'm sorry to disappoint you," she said with false politeness, watching the leaping anger that flared in his eyes, "but I have no intention of moving. This is my home and nothing you can say or do is going to drive me away."

Grant stared at her with brooding savagery, the slitted gray eyes glittering with suppressed emotion. Mara received the distinct impression that he could have cheerfully throttled her, and when he took a jerky step forward she stiffened, bracing herself for his attack.

The action seemed to bring him to his senses, and he came to a halt, the shuttered look dropping over his face again. "I'll have Vicky contact you about the portrait," he said tersely. Face set, he stepped past her and marched toward the door.

When it slammed behind him, Mara remained where she was for several seconds, staring blankly at nothing. The bereft, empty feeling settled over her again, and she shivered, feeling suddenly cold.

Why did this nagging guilt eat at her? So she'd made him angry. So what? He had no business interfering in her life. Mara sat down and unzipped her boots and pulled them off, then curled herself into the corner of the sofa. With her elbow on the armrest, she propped her chin in her hand and fixed her eyes on the cold ashes in the fireplace. Maybe after tonight, Grant would leave her alone. She certainly intended to give him a wide berth.

Chapter Seven

"I think we'll call it a day."

Mara wiped her brush on a rag and swished it through the turpentine bath. From the corner of her eye she saw Vicky unwind from her cramped position and arch her back, sighing as the tight muscles relaxed. A vague uneasiness gnawed at Mara as she watched her. Vicky always looked wistful and rather sad, but that day her unhappiness seemed almost overpowering, her blue eyes deep pools of longing. Mara sighed too. She wanted very much to help in some way, but so far Vicky had not confided in her.

They had been working on the portrait for over a week now. During that time they'd talked quite a lot, but Mara sensed that Vicky was holding something back. For the past hour she had been distracted and fidgety. Something was obviously troubling her.

Vicky wandered over to the glass wall and stood staring out at the forest. Mara's eyes followed her worriedly.

"Just give me a few minutes to clean these brushes and I'll be ready to go," she said, crossing to the utility sink. "I can hardly wait for a cup of your mother's delicious coffee."

"Mmmmm," Vicky answered absently.

Shaking her head, Mara continued with her cleaning. Maybe Vicky's mother could cheer her up.

Mara had been apprehensive about meeting Mrs. Ridgeway, but she needn't have been. Grant and Vicky's mother was a charming, warm woman. Unlike her son, she had accepted Mara at face value and, amazingly, an instant rapport had sprung up between them. The day Mara had started the portrait, Alice Ridgeway had insisted that they join her for coffee after the sitting, and now it had become a part of their daily routine.

"Was your husband older than you, Mara?"

The question came from out of the blue, and Mara threw her a curious look, wondering what had prompted it. But Vicky still stood with her back to the room, staring out of the window.

"Yes. Six years. Why do you ask?"

"Oh, I just wondered." Vicky turned and gave Mara a wan smile. "Do you think a marriage can be successful if there's a large age difference between husband and wife?"

"I suppose it would depend on the two people involved," Mara replied cautiously. There was more behind this conversation than just idle curiosity. Vicky was working up to something. Mara was sure of it.

"But you do agree that if two people love each other, I mean *really* love each other, an age difference shouldn't present a problem, don't you?" Vicky asked with gentle persistence.

"I suppose so."

Flopping down on the chaise lounge, Vicky released a long, aggrieved sigh. "I just wish I could get Grant to agree that easily."

A knowing smile tugged at the corners of Mara's mouth. The pieces of the puzzle were finally fitting together. After stacking the brushes in the drying rack, she walked over to the chaise lounge and sat down beside the dejected girl. "I gather from all this that you're in love with an older man, and your brother doesn't approve. Am I right?"

Vicky turned desolate, tear-drenched eyes on her. "Oh, Mara," she breathed through quivering lips. "I love him so much. What am I going to do?"

"First of all, you're going to tell me who we're talking about and why Grant doesn't like him."

"Oh, but Grant does like him! In fact, they're the best of friends. Eric and Grant practically grew up together." Vicky paused, then added wretchedly, "And I've been in love with him since I was ten years old."

"I see. And does Eric love you?"

"Yes," Vicky stated quickly, with a touch of defiance. Then her tone altered, her voice dropping to a hesitant whisper. "At least . . . I think so. I know he asked Grant for permission to date me. But Grant wouldn't hear of it. He said I was too young and the age difference was too great."

"And just how old is Eric?"

"Thirty-six. The same as Grant."

Mara's brows rose. Thirty-six to Vicky's eighteen. That was quite a difference. No wonder her brother objected. Still, she knew of several successful marriages with worse handicaps. Perhaps Vicky needed someone older. Because her father had died when she was small, Grant had been the masculine role model in her life. It was possible she was unconsciously seeking the same type of man for a husband, someone strong enough and mature enough to measure up to her brother's image.

"Well, Vicky, you *are* of age, you know. You don't really need Grant's permission to date Eric," Mara suggested boldly. She ignored the flutter in the pit of her stomach. There would be hell to pay if Grant ever found out she'd encouraged his sister to rebel against him, but she hated to see Vicky so unhappy.

Vicky's eyes filled with tears. She blinked hard, trying to hold them back, but they began to trickle slowly down her cheeks. "I know, but don't you see? Eric likes and respects Grant too much to go against his wishes," she cried miserably, choking off a sob.

"What does your mother say about all this?"

Vicky scrubbed away the escaping tears with the back of her hand. "Oh, Mother won't cross Grant either. She says he's the man of the family and we must trust his judgement."

Remembering the snap judgements he'd made about her, Mara didn't find that argument too impressive. With a sigh, she picked up Vicky's hand and gave it a consoling pat. "I'm sorry, dear. I wish there was something I could do to help you."

"Thanks." Vicky gave her a watery smile and sniffed. "It helps a little just to be able to talk about it."

"I'm available anytime." Rising to her feet, Mara added in a brisk tone, "Now then. I think we'd better make tracks, or your mother will think we've forgotten her."

But later, as she sat sipping coffee with Vicky and Alice Ridgeway in front of the fireplace in Grant's large, comfortable living room, Mara had difficulty keeping her mind on the conversation. Vicky's revelations had unsettled her. She felt torn in two directions. On the one hand she could understand Grant's attitude. Vicky was very young, even younger, emotionally, than most girls her age. She had been sheltered and protected all her life, and Grant was merely continuing that pattern. Yet he really didn't have the right to make such a major decision for her. True, his protests were legitimate. Eric *was* too old for her. But surely Grant realized that people didn't fall in love to order. When it happened, it happened. And there was very little mere mortals could do about it. For just a moment Mara considered approaching him on Vicky's behalf, but she rejected the idea almost immediately. Considering the way Grant felt about her, it was unlikely he'd take her advice. She'd probably do more harm than good.

A telephone ringing in the distance broke into her thoughts. With determination, Mara forced her mind back to the feminine conversation swirling around her.

". . . think that would be best. Don't you agree, Mara?" Alice Ridgeway asked.

Thanksgiving was less than a week away, and Mara had been invited to share the traditional feast. Vicky and Alice had been discussing what to serve and organizing their work schedules in order to have time to help prepare the huge meal, but Mara had lost the thread of the conversation several minutes ago. She gave the older woman a blank look.

"I'm sorry, I . . ."

"Vicky, you're wanted on the phone." Grant's deep voice interrupted whatever apology Mara had been about to make, and three heads turned to see him framed in the doorway.

"I'll take it in my room," Vicky said, heading for the door.

Alice's gray eyes lit up when they encountered her son. She was a tall, regal-looking woman whose elegant beauty could not be diminished by years. The silver hair and softly wrinkled skin merely added dignity to the face that was a feminine version of her son's.

She smiled at him warmly. "Hello, dear. I didn't realize you had returned. Why don't you come in and join us? The coffee is still hot."

Grant's gaze flicked to Mara, then back. A muscle

tensed in his jaw. "No, thanks. I have a lot of paper work
to catch up on." The flat refusal brooked no argument.
Without another word, he pivoted on his heel and disappeared.

Mara pulled her eyes away from the empty doorway,
feeling oddly hurt as she listened to the heavy thud of his
boot heels fading down the hall.

"Don't let it worry you, my dear," Alice said softly,
and Mara glanced up, surprised to find herself the object
of a sympathetic look. "Grant is behaving like a bear with
a sore paw because, deep down, he knows he's misjudged
you. He just can't bring himself to admit it, that's all. I'm
afraid he got that stiff-necked pride from me." Alice
smiled. "And don't look so surprised. I'm well aware of
my son's unreasonable attitude toward you. But if you'll
just be patient a little longer, I'm sure he'll work it out."

"Grant doesn't bother me, Alice." Mara sipped her
coffee, but it had grown cold. Leaning over, she placed
the half-full cup on the low table.

"Please try to understand, my dear. Grant had to learn
at a very early age to shoulder responsibilities and trust his
own judgement, and I must admit, my son is a very
shrewd judge of character." She paused and gave Mara a
long, penetrating look. "But in your case I'm afraid he
allowed past hurts to blind him to the truth. You're
nothing at all like your aunt."

Shock hit Mara like a dash of cold water in the face.
"You *know?*" The question burst out in a breathless
whisper. She couldn't believe it! All this time she had
carefully avoided any mention of her aunt, not wanting to
hurt Alice and afraid of damaging the new and fragile
friendship that had sprung up between them. And all
along her caution had been unnecessary.

"Yes, my dear. I know. Actually, Grant himself gave it
away." Alice's gray eyes twinkled as they traveled over

Mara's shapely figure. "You see, my son usually tries to seduce beautiful women."

Taken aback by the blunt statement, Mara's brows shot upward. No doubt Alice was right. His rugged masculinity probably drew women like flies. He'd have no difficulty satisfying his male appetites, of that she was certain, although it was a little disconcerting to hear that opinion expressed so openly by his mother.

Alice laughed delightedly. "Don't look so shocked. My son is very discreet, but he makes no secret of the fact that he enjoys . . . uh . . . feminine company. That's how I knew something was wrong. His behavior toward you was completely out of character. So I did some snooping. It took very little effort on my part to discover that you were Enid's niece."

"And you don't mind?"

"Of course not! Heavens! None of us can choose our relatives. Only our friends." Alice paused and smiled. Gray eyes met green ones, their message clear and direct, and Mara felt as though a great load had been lifted from her shoulders. "I'd very much like us to be friends, Mara."

"I'd like that too."

Leaning forward, Alice picked up Mara's hand and gave it a gentle pat. "My dear, I hope you'll be patient with Grant and not judge him too harshly. Please believe me when I tell you he's not been himself for the past few months. Normally he's a very warm, considerate man." Seeing Mara's skeptical expression, Alice's mouth tilted in a rueful smile. "It's quite true, I assure you."

She sighed, her eyes growing sad. "His father's desertion hurt us both, but Grant especially. Fifteen is such a vulnerable, impressionable age for a boy. In most instances, Grant is a fair-minded, reasonable man, but where I'm concerned he has a blind spot. You see, I loved my first husband very much, and when he left me for Enid I was devastated. Grant has never forgotten that. Since then he's been fiercely protective of me. There's nothing he won't do, nothing he won't sacrifice, including his own happiness, to spare me further pain.''

Alice gave Mara a regretful look. "I suppose when he discovered, as I did, that as a child you had spent your summers with Enid, he assumed you were like her. Then, of course, your being an artist merely strengthened his assumption.''

"What do you mean?''

"Only that Grant remembers Enid very well. Years ago she had a small weekend cabin on her land, on the spot where your house is located. She and a bunch of her artist friends used to come here now and then. Their wild parties shocked the locals, I can tell you. Actually, that was how Richard met her. He was so incensed that he went over there to complain about the noise and the shocking behavior of her guests. The next thing I knew, they were involved in a full-blown affair. One night, during a particularly wild party, the cabin was burned to the ground. When Enid was forced to return to Houston, Richard went with her.'' Alice's eyes had a faraway look, remembered pain flickering briefly in their smoky gray depths. "A year later when she grew tired of him and threw him out, he couldn't face his family and friends. He became a drifter, a bum.''

Mara's grip tightened around the older woman's hand. "I'm so sorry, Alice,'' she whispered, her voice rough with emotion.

"Don't let it trouble you, my dear. I got over it all a long time ago, with Tom Ridgeway's help. When we received word of Richard's death, nine years after he had disappeared, all I could feel was a deep sadness for a life wasted. I couldn't even cry. My love for him was totally dead.''

"The past no longer has the power to hurt me, but I've not been able to convince my son of that. He'll go to any lengths to shield and protect both Vicky and me. And I'm quite sure when he finally falls in love he'll be equally possessive and protective toward the woman of his choice. Unlike his father, once committed, Grant's loyalty and fidelity are unswerving."

Mara laughed softly. "Alice, you just told me your son's a bit of a ladies' man. Somehow the two images just don't match."

"Nonsense!" Alice brushed aside the observation with a wave of her hand. "I've yet to meet a real man who didn't sow a few wild oats in his youth. It means nothing." She picked up her cup and took a sip of coffee. Her face wore a soft, dreamy look. "When my son meets the right woman she'll be his whole existence, and believe me, he'll want a lasting relationship. Nothing else would do for a man like Grant."

Lasting. Was there such a thing? Mara wondered silently. In her experience there hadn't been, especially when it came to something as intangible and ephemeral as human emotions. Life was short; people came and went in the blink of an eye. It was best not to build too many hopes and dreams around them.

There was a biting chill in the air as Mara walked home through the thick woods. A heavy frost had painted the trees with vivid autumn colors, a riot of brilliant reds and yellows, deep, rich purples and magentas. A squirrel scurried up a tall pine tree, busily stashing his winter food supply. On the other side of the small creek a deer bounded away through the bracken, its white tail held aloft like a flag. But for once the beauty of nature held no interest for Mara.

With her hands in the pockets of her heavy, fleece-lined jacket she held the front edges together and followed the narrow trail through the woods. Her eyes were on the path, but her mind was far away. She was introspective by nature, but that day Mara was so caught up in the complicated maze of her own thoughts that nothing else registered. She had learned a lot about her neighbors, perhaps more than she wanted to know. The reason for Vicky's haunted look was now clear. Mara's heart went out to the girl and she longed to help her, but as far as she could see there was nothing she could do.

During the course of her conversation with Alice, her impression of Grant had altered. He now seemed more real, more vulnerable, more human, somehow, and Mara wasn't sure she liked that. It seemed safer to keep him at a distance, to see him as a cold, unfeeling autocrat with no redeeming qualities.

A thick carpet of red and gold leaves covered the trail, rustling softly underfoot as Mara strolled along. She kicked at them absently while her thoughts continued to twist and turn. If she had learned a lot that day, she had also revealed a lot. Without knowing quite how it had come about, she had found herself opening up to Alice, telling her things she had revealed to no one else but David. Slowly, painfully at first, and then with a growing sense of relief, she had told of her parents' disastrous marriage and her lonely, isolated childhood, of her father's neglect and her aunt's indifference, of her years of hard work, of the intense love she and David had shared, and finally, of the painful, crushing grief she had suffered when he died. Once started, it had all come pouring out of her in a rush, and she had been unable to stop until it was all said. Through it all Alice listened—really listened. When Mara was finished, she knew she had added a new person to her small circle of friends.

The minute she entered the house, Mara climbed the stairs to the studio. She felt stirred up and restless, her emotional balance upset, and the best tranquilizer she knew was painting. When she worked she could shut off her mind to everything. Every feeling, every thought was channeled into her painting.

Mara removed Vicky's unfinished portrait from the studio easel and replaced it with a large landscape that she had been doing off and on for the past week. Two or three more hours' work and it would be finished. She laid out the colors she would need and picked up a brush. Within five minutes her mind was free of everything but the picture before her.

She had painted steadily for two hours before she became aware of the tiny flashes of light behind her eyes. Her head was throbbing, and the pressure had already begun to build up in the back of her head, but she ignored it. She needed only a few more minutes to finish. Gritting her teeth against the increasing pain, Mara forced herself to continue.

But it was no use. Her concentration was shot. Perspiration broke out on her forehead as the searing agony intensified. It felt as if someone was driving hot nails into her skull. Accepting defeat, Mara swished her brushes through the turpentine bath and turned toward the sink. She stumbled across the floor and gripped the edge of the counter, gasping for breath as wave upon wave of nausea washed over her. Oh, God! Why had she waited so long? She knew she had to get to the phone and call a doctor. It was too late now to take the tablets.

Taking a deep breath, Mara turned toward the stairs, took two staggering steps, then fell to the floor, her knees buckling under her. She hit the hardwood floor with a loud thud but didn't even feel the pain. Compared with the torture going on inside her head, it was nothing.

Whimpering softly, Mara crawled on her hands and knees toward the top of the stairs. Perspiration beaded her white face as she forced her trembling limbs forward, red dots of pain exploding in her head with every move. It was sheer agony every inch of the way, but finally, *finally,* she made it. After maneuvering around to a sitting position on the top step, she began to ease herself down, slowly and carefully, one step at a time. Her eyes were closed and she was gritting her teeth, fighting to control the churning sickness in her stomach. Short, tight cries of pain broke from her throat with every breath.

The loud knocking on the front door didn't register. Mara slid down another step and moaned when the movement jarred her head. Another knock sounded. After a short pause, the door was thrust open.

"Mara, where are . . . What the *hell!"*

There was a loud, clumping noise as someone took the steps two at a time.

"Mara! Mara, what's wrong?" Strong hands clasped her shoulders, halting her feeble progress, and she cried out against the pain. "My God! What is it? You look like death." Grant's voice held a mixture of shock and deep concern. He slipped his arm around her shoulders and cupped her face with his other hand. "Tell me, Mara. What is it?" he questioned roughly, urgently, his frantic eyes running over her upturned face.

Mara struggled to answer him. "My . . . my . . . head." She stopped to bite her lip. "Oh, God! I'm going to be sick!"

Everything was a whirling blur as Grant scooped her up in his arms and carried her down the stairs. She closed her eyes and clung to him, moaning in protest. In the bathroom he lowered her gently and held her head while she was violently ill, her body shuddering. When the appalling sickness was over he carefully wiped her stiff, white face with a cold cloth, gave her a cup of water so that she could swish out her mouth, and then lifted her in his arms and carried her into the bedroom.

Mara lay on the bed, shivering and cold with reaction, still fighting the unbearable pain in her head. Dimly, she was aware that Grant had left the room. Don't leave me! her mind cried out. But she was too weak to voice the words. Tears trickled from beneath her closed eyelids. She hurt so badly and felt so alone. So alone.

Grant came back into the room. "I've called my doctor. He'll be here in a few minutes," he said, staring down at her huddled figure.

Mara tried to look back at him, but he kept wavering sickeningly, like someone seen through distorted glass. She moaned and closed her eyes again. The heavy weight of a comforter settled over her. Gentle hands tucked the soft covering under her chin and close against the sides of her body.

A few minutes later she heard Grant rummaging around in the bathroom. When he came back he placed a cold, wet cloth across her forehead, and Mara sighed with pleasure. But the relief was only temporary. Within a few seconds the pain was back, even stronger. She began to twist and writhe, harsh, agonized sounds tearing from her throat.

Grant sat down on the edge of the bed and smoothed the hair away from her face. "Mara, Mara," he breathed worriedly. "Just hang on, sweetheart. Dr. Jamison will be here soon."

The next few minutes seemed like hours. Mara existed on the edge of a black void. The excruciating pain in her head was almost more than she could endure, yet the blessed release of unconsciousness remained just out of reach.

She knew the doctor had arrived when she became aware of a strange masculine voice mingling with Grant's.

"How long has she been this way?" The calm query was issued as a stethoscope was pressed against her chest.

"I don't know. She was like this when I arrived, about twenty minutes ago," Grant replied. "She was sick right after that, and she seems to be getting steadily worse. I think it's a migraine.'' There was a short pause and then the rattle of a pill bottle. "I found these in the medicine cabinet.''

Mara stirred. She heard their voices and understood every word. She wanted to tell them how she felt but couldn't force the words out.

"Mmmmm. Yes, it's migraine all right. This is a strong pain killer, specifically for that ailment, but she's too far gone for this to be of any help now. I'll have to give her an injection. Someone must stay with her, however. This will knock her out cold for several hours, and there's danger of suffocating if she turns in her sleep.''

"Don't worry. I'm not going to leave her,'' Grant told him firmly.

Mara was almost hysterical with relief. She had been so afraid they wouldn't know what was wrong with her, or what to do for it. She had meant to visit the local doctor and explain about her headaches but just hadn't gotten around to it, somehow. It had been so long since she'd had a migraine it was quite easy to put the problem out of her mind.

There was a tiny stinging prick in her arm; then the comforter was being tucked back under her chin. The low murmur of voices began to fade. Mara's hand groped out from under the cover, reaching out blindly.

"Don't . . . leave . . . me.'' It was a soft, fearful plea, barely audible, but immediately a large hand enfolded hers.

"Don't worry, sweetheart. I won't leave you.''

Mara opened her eyes and blinked. It was dark, but a long rectangle of light spilled through the open door from the living room, creating a soft glow. Very carefully she turned her head to look at the clock and was startled to find Grant sitting in the wing-backed chair beside the bed.

He smiled and cocked one brow. "Feeling better?''

She stared at him for a moment, speechless. "What are you doing here?"

"Don't you remember last night?"

"Last night?" Mara repeated vaguely. Then it all came rushing back. She put a hand to her head and touched it gingerly. "Oh yes. I had a headache."

"That's the understatement of the year," he muttered.

Mara gave him a curious look. "Don't tell me you've been here all night?" The bedside clock drew her eyes, and she gasped. "Why, it's three in the morning!"

"Yes." He smiled. "You've been sleeping like a baby for the last ten hours."

That unnerved her. Had he been sitting there all that time, watching her sleep? She started to sit up, then stopped short as she realized that she was naked beneath the cover. A frantic grab brought the sheet back up under her armpits, but the satin comforter slithered down to her waist. Her wide, astonished eyes sought Grant's. "Did you . . . I mean . . . " She bit her lip and looked away, her face flaming.

"Yes, I undressed you—if that's what you're trying to ask." His eyes dropped from her averted face to her shoulders, then down to where her full breasts thrust against the thin sheet. The hint of a smile in his voice deepened Mara's flush. "I didn't think you'd want to sleep in your clothes. I did consider putting a nightgown on you, but after seeing those filmy things in your dresser, I didn't see much point."

Mara closed her eyes, consumed with embarrassment. Good Lord! The man had not only seen her naked, he'd gone through her most intimate apparel as well!

"Don't look so stricken, Mara. You have a very beautiful body and absolutely nothing to be ashamed of."

Something in his tone made her eyes fly open, and she stared at him. His warm, intent expression made her uneasy. Her gaze dropped to where her fingers were nervously creasing tiny pleats in the sheet. She had to say something—anything to break the strained silence.

"I . . . I'm sorry to have put you to so much trouble. It really wasn't necessary for you to sit up with me all night."

"How long have you had these headaches?" he questioned with soft determination.

Very carefully, Mara sat up, clutching the sheet to her with one hand as she adjusted the pillows behind her back. "Oh, I don't know. Most of my adult life, I guess. They're brought on by tension or emotional strain." Mara saw no point in telling him that during her marriage the headaches had all but disappeared. They had been happy, carefree years, the happiest of her life, but when they ended the headaches had returned immediately. During the past two years they had occurred more frequently, and with more severity, than ever before.

"I see," Grant murmured thoughtfully. "Tell me—the first day I met you, had you suffered a headache the night before?"

"Yes." She frowned. "I thought I explained that."

"No. You did mention something about pills, but I'm afraid I misunderstood." He reached over and picked up the prescription bottle from the bedside table. "These are the pills you were referring to?"

Mara glanced at the bottle and made a face. "Yes. I hate to take them, but sometimes I have no choice."

Grant's mouth firmed into a grim line. Replacing the bottle on the table, he stood up abruptly and looked down at her for a long moment. "I've really misjudged you, haven't I, Mara?"

Mara transferred her gaze to her busy fingers and remained silent. She recalled how tender he'd been with her while she'd been so wretchedly ill, and how quickly he'd gotten help. She didn't want to quarrel with him. Not now.

When he saw she wasn't going to answer, to her surprise he sat down on the edge of the bed and picked up both her hands, halting their plucking movements. "I'm sorry, Mara. I was so positive you were a cold, selfish little tramp, just like your aunt, that I refused to see what was right before my eyes." The self-contempt in his voice was unmistakable.

Mara looked up, surprised. The strange, tender expression on his face caused her heart to thump crazily.

"But you're nothing like that," he said softly, almost as though he were talking to himself. His gaze wandered over her upturned face. "You're a giving, generous, thoughtful person."

His thumbs stroked absently over the backs of her hands. Mara wanted to pull away but dared not. After all, he was only trying to apologize.

The drug-induced sleep had left her groggy and dim-witted, but slowly, surely, certain things were beginning to penetrate the thick fog that surrounded her. She was very conscious of Grant's muscled thigh pressed against her hip, the warmth of his body, the clean, intoxicating male scent of him. Her senses were responding to his nearness and the evocative intimacy of the situation in an alarming manner. Awareness of Grant's potent masculinity coursed through her, and she shivered.

Grant's hands were slowly working their way up her arms, stroking and kneading the soft flesh on their way. He was watching her through half-closed eyes, his look warm and sensuous. "I find it amazing that such a warm, vibrant creature could have emerged from that loveless environment," he murmured as his hands massaged the rounded curves of her shoulders.

Mara's eyes flew to his face, her distress evident in their green depths. "What are you talking about?" But a sickening premonition was already clawing at her. Grant raised a hand and ran his knuckles down the smooth curve of her cheek and jaw, but she barely noticed. She was too intent on his answer.

"Mother told me about your childhood, Mara." His voice was low and tender, his eyes a soft, gray velvet.

"She had no right!" Mara stared at him in horror, a bank of unshed tears blurring his image. She couldn't believe that the woman she'd been so sure was her friend had betrayed her. And to Grant, of all people. "I told her those things in strictest confidence. She had no right to tell you," she repeated, her voice shaking with bitterness.

Mara usually avoided relating her past history to anyone. Inevitably people reacted in one of two ways. They either smothered her with pity or looked at her askance, as though wondering what flaw she possessed that made it impossible for anyone to love her. She found both reactions humiliating.

"Maybe not. But Mother thought I should know."

Mutely, Mara shook her head in resentful denial. She was too close to tears to speak.

His hands cupped her face, his fingers thrusting into her hair. "Oh, Mara." Grant breathed her name like a caress. "Don't you see? I *needed* to know." He leaned forward, and Mara's heart slammed against her ribs as she read the message in his eyes.

She wanted to thrust him away, to shout at him to stop, but the words wouldn't come. She was too panic-stricken. Her heart pounding wildly, she watched his slowly descending mouth, her gaze caught like that of a mesmerized rabbit.

Grant's lips met hers with an excruciating tenderness that made her quiver. It was a gentle, devouring kiss, his mouth sipping at hers, savoring each taste.

Mara felt perspiration spring out all over her, her skin tingling with a feverish excitement as his questing tongue explored the shape of her mouth. The blood sang in her ears. She shivered violently, desire surging through her veins like a molten lava flow. If he had been brutal, or even aggressive, she could have resisted him. But he wasn't. He was giving her just what she needed, what had been missing from her life for the past two years, what she craved more than anything else: tenderness and a warm, loving touch. It was like giving water to a man dying of thirst in the desert, and she reacted to it instinctively, reaching out with both hands to hold him close.

Grant immediately deepened the kiss, the hard tip of his tongue coaxing her lips apart and slipping into the warm, moist sweetness of her mouth. A soft moan of pleasure escaped Mara's throat, and his tongue plunged deeper, stroking and probing with an ardent passion that left her weak. Helplessly, Mara threaded her fingers through his thick, black hair, exploring the shape of his head while she returned his kiss with equal fervor.

Grant's hands slipped downward to her breasts. He shoved aside the sheet and cupped a warm, firm globe in each palm. His supple fingers kneaded the silky flesh gently, caressingly, as his thumbs traced erotic patterns over the rosy crests. As he felt them harden under his touch, he tore his mouth away from hers and buried his face in the side of her neck.

"Mara, Mara," Grant breathed unevenly. She lay with her head thrown back, allowing him to feast on her skin, his lips gliding and nibbling their way to the base of her neck, over her shoulder and down to the pearly glimmer of her breasts. For just a moment he rested his face in the scented valley, then turned his head, and with his mouth open, breathed a hot, moist trail up over the creamy slope and took possession of the aroused peak. He rolled the hard button with his tongue for a moment; then his lips took over. Mara drew in a hissing breath, her body arching upward in response to the gentle tugging pressure, her hands roaming in frantic exploration over his back and shoulders. It had been so long since she had felt a man's loving touch. So very long.

He began to shake. She felt his convulsive movements and moaned in sympathetic agreement. Then his mouth closed over hers again, and the fiery kiss set off a raging inferno that threatened to blaze out of control.

The strident ring of the phone on the bedside table tore them apart. Grant shook his head and stared at it, dazed. Finally he reached out and snatched up the offending instrument.

"Yes," he demanded in a husky, disturbed voice. His breathing was an audible rasp in the quiet room.

Mara lay in the bed staring at his harsh profile with huge, stricken eyes. Her face was white. *Oh my God! What have I done?* She had allowed Grant, a man who didn't even like her, to hold her and kiss her, to intimately caress her body! *Had she lost her mind?* Shivering with self-disgust, Mara pulled the sheet up to her chin and pressed her balled fist to her mouth. How could she have done that? How *could* she?

Slowly, Mara became aware that Grant had grown rigid beside her, that his face had stiffened in cold fury, and that he was looking down at her with absolute loathing.

"Yes. She's here. Just one moment." Removing the receiver from his ear, he covered the mouthpiece with his other hand and raked her with a cold, contemptuous stare.

"Please allow me to repeat the apology I made earlier, Mrs. Whitcomb," he said smoothly, the nasty sneer in his voice canceling out the polite words. "I was wrong about you"—he paused, his voice hardening—"in every way but one." Standing up, he tossed the receiver onto the bed. "It's your lover," he spat out in disgust, then turned and started for the door.

"Lover?" Mara gazed at Grant's stiff, retreating form, not even aware that she had repeated the word.

At the door Grant turned. ''Who else would call you in the middle of the night?''

Chuck, that's who, she thought instantly, but before she could answer he was gone.

Mara heard his long, furious strides cross the living room. Then the front door was slammed shut with a force that rattled the windows. In the silence that followed she heard the small, distant sound of Chuck's voice yelling through the receiver. With a glance at the clock and a resigned sigh, Mara picked it up.

Chapter Eight

"Yes, Chuck. What is it?"

"Who the hell was that?" he growled. "It sounded like that damned cowboy. Look here, Mara, if he's been over there bothering you again, I'll . . ."

"Grant wasn't bothering me, Chuck." At least, not in the way you think, she amended silently, wincing as she heard Grant's car roar down the drive.

"If he wasn't bothering you, then what was he doing there? Do you realize it's almost four in the morning?"

"*I* realize it. Do you?" she asked dryly.

There was a short pause. "Well, yes . . . of course I do," Chuck answered, in a somewhat mollified tone. "Now that I've looked at the clock." Realizing he'd blundered once again, he chuckled wickedly. Then, in the middle of it, Mara heard him suck in a deep breath. "*Saaay.*" The word was stretched out into a long, incredulous sound. "Don't tell me you and Mr. Macho have a thing going?"

"Certainly not! Grant just happened to come by yester-

128

day while I was having one of my headaches. He called the doctor, then stayed with me while I slept it off. That's all!'' Mara's voice was sharp and acid-tipped. Her anger was out of proportion and she knew it, but that sizzling scene with Grant was still too fresh in her mind.

"Oh, love, I'm sorry,'' Chuck returned quickly. "Thank God *someone* was there.'' The genuine concern in his voice pricked at Mara's conscience, and her face softened. Her anger had just begun to melt away when he continued in a harder tone. "Helen and I tried to tell you not to move out there all by yourself. This is exactly the sort of thing we were worried about.''

"Chuck,'' she hissed warningly, "did you call just to lecture me, or did you have something to say?''

That brought him up short, and after a moment of silence he said sheepishly, "Sorry, love. I didn't mean to sound like a heavy-handed big brother. It's just that we love you and . . .''

"I know, Chuck. I know.'' Massaging away the frown line between her brows, Mara sighed and leaned forward to prop her elbows on her bent knees, cupping her hand across her forehead. She hadn't meant to take out her guilt and frustration on Chuck. It was hardly his fault. A quick rake of her parted fingers pushed the tangle of bright hair away from her face. She drew a deep breath and forced a lighter note into her voice. "Now, tell me. Why *did* you call?''

"Oh, yeah. Helen wanted me to call you. She had to fly to New Orleans on family business and the thing is, she won't be able to get back until the day before the wedding. She wanted me to ask if you'd mind picking up her wedding dress at Neiman's. They promised to have it ready by Monday. For some reason, she didn't trust me to pick it up,'' he added in an aggrieved tone.

"Wise girl, our Helen,'' Mara drawled.

"Good grief! I'm already beginning to feel like a

married man. Only I have *two* women giving me a hard time.''

"Don't worry about it, my friend. Come Wednesday, I relinquish all nagging rights. From then on, you're going to be Helen's responsibility.''

"Yeah.'' Chuck sighed dreamily, as though he found the prospect enchanting.

After assuring him that she would pick up the dress, Mara replaced the receiver and lay back against the pillows, her face pensive. That whole scene with Grant had unsettled her, and she knew she wouldn't rest until she'd taken it out and examined it and rooted out the cause of her uncharacteristic behavior.

She had never responded so wantonly to any man but David. Even with him it had been months before she had really let herself go—not until she was sure of his love for her and hers for him. For Mara, a purely physical relationship had never been enough. Her very soul rebelled against it, needing the security of love before she could respond freely. She had assumed it would always be so.

Mara stirred restlessly on the bed, her mind probing at the problem, refusing to rest until it was solved. That night she had responded eagerly to Grant's tender passion, and she realized now that it had been his very gentleness that had been her undoing. His unhurried, considerate loving reminding her so poignantly of all that she'd had—all that she'd lost. Strangely, despite Alice and Vicky's claims to the contrary, Mara had believed Grant to be a cold, unfeeling man. It came as a shock to realize that he could be every bit as tender and caring as David had been.

She had always known that Grant was fiercely protective of the women in his family, but now she saw that he possessed an old-fashioned chivalrous attitude toward all women. Hadn't he come to her aid the night her car had broken down, and hadn't he expressed concern over her safety on several occasions? He didn't like her, but she was female, and therefore he felt obligated to protect her, insofar as he could.

After much soul-searching, Mara finally came to the conclusion that the night's fiasco was largely her fault. Having learned the truth about her, Grant had come over to apologize, and finding her ill and in pain had probably added to his sense of guilt. She was sure he had only intended to comfort her, but she had caught fire in his arms, and Mara was well aware that any normal, red-blooded male could lose control when he found himself holding a naked, willing woman.

Mara sighed heavily. It was going to be embarrassing, facing Grant again, but face him she must. Alice and Vicky were expecting her for Thanksgiving, and she wasn't about to let the night's mistake spoil their friendship.

Suddenly Mara was very glad she had agreed to stay with the Mercers for the next few days to help with the preparations for Chuck and Helen's wedding. Maybe by the time I return Grant will have cooled down and dismissed the whole stupid incident from his mind, she told herself hopefully as she watched the cool gray light of dawn ease the shadows from the room.

Pop! The champagne cork went flying across the room, amid gales of laughter from the bride and groom and the small party of wedding guests. Chuck carefully filled two delicate, long-stemmed glasses with the bubbly liquid. He picked them up and handed one to his bride. His eyes glowed with adoration as they clinked together.

"To the love of my life. For now and always," he said tenderly, and Helen blushed like a schoolgirl.

Watching them, Mara was choked with emotion, her chin quivering. Happy tears filled her eyes, and she had to blink rapidly to keep them from spilling over. As the waiters passed among the small group with trays of filled glasses, she sniffed and swallowed to ease the painful constriction of her throat. She took a glass from one of the trays, and when Helen's father proposed a toast to the newlyweds, dutifully raised it to her lips and took a sip. For Helen and Chuck she would even set aside her abhorrence for alcohol.

Glancing around the beautiful, elegant living room, she smiled. The haunting sadness she usually felt when she was in this house had all but disappeared, and she was glad. It was a lovely place, meant for laughter and happiness—not tears. The Mercers, bless them, had insisted on hosting the reception, and Helen and Chuck had been delighted with the idea, since this was where they'd met.

Except for Helen's relatives, who had flown in from New Orleans, Mara knew most of the guests and circulated freely. She spent a few minutes talking to Joe and Freda Thorn and was relieved to learn that they were delighted with their new son-in-law. Chuck, it seemed, was as opposite from Helen's first husband as it was possible to be, which suited her parents just fine.

The reception continued for another hour, but it was not until the end, just before they left to catch their flight to the Bahamas, that Mara had a chance to speak to her friends alone.

She had gone into the bedroom with Helen to help her change into her traveling suit. They had barely finished before Chuck was pounding on the door.

"Hurry up, you two. If we don't leave soon we'll miss our plane."

Mara opened the door just wide enough to pull him inside. "For heaven's sake, Chuck! Will you pipe down! You have plenty of time." She gave him a disgusted look. "You're embarrassing Helen with your boorish behavior.

I think it's positively obscene, the way you're in such a hurry to get this poor girl alone. What's the matter with you? Don't you have any decency, any manners?'' Helen giggled as Mara struggled to keep a straight face.

Chuck grinned unabashedly. ''What do I need manners for? I'm a married man now,'' he said with a smirk, and Mara gave him a quick poke in the ribs.

She sighed and sent Helen a pitying look. ''You're not getting much of a bargain, you know.''

''I know. But someone has to look after this big, dumb lummox.'' Helen assumed a look of resigned martyrdom, and they all laughed.

Then it really was time to go. Helen and Mara embraced, half laughing, half crying. When they finally drew apart, Mara turned to Chuck and was immediately engulfed in one of his huge bear hugs. She hugged him back, biting her trembling lips as tears trickled from beneath her tightly closed lids. Finally she stepped back, still holding his hands.

''You take good care of her, Chuck Ainsley,'' she said shakily. Her gaze swung to include Helen. ''And remember, I love you both.''

The formal dining room in Grant's home had a festive air. From the flickering candles on the sideboard came the pleasing scent of bayberry. Fine china, flatware, and crystal adorned the linen-covered table, and in the center there was a lush arrangement of bronze and gold chrysanthemums, flanked by silver candelabras. The table fairly groaned under the weight of the lavish feast, which included turkey and dressing, candied yams, cranberry sauce, several different vegetables and salads, and a choice of rolls or cornbread. Pecan, pumpkin, and mincemeat pies sat on the sideboard for those who had the capacity for dessert.

In addition to Mara, there were four other guests:

Grant's friend Eric Delany and Janice Holman and her parents. Alice Ridgeway and Nora Holman, a plump, matronly woman in her mid-fifties, had been friends since their college days, Mara had learned earlier.

Janice's high-pitched laughter broke into the murmur of voices, and Mara looked up, catching Vicky's eye. The disgruntled expression on her young friend's face caused Mara to smile and hurriedly look away. Janice was not one of Vicky's favorite people. She had made that much plain on several occasions.

Mara had been amused by Janice's possessive attitude toward Grant and the warning looks the blonde had thrown her way. The woman's jealousy was really comical, considering the way things were between Grant and herself. When she had come face to face with him that morning he had snapped a curt "Hello" and promptly retreated to his study until the others arrived and had barely spoken two words to her since. It was clear, as far as Grant was concerned, that they were back to square one.

"How long have you lived here, Mara?" Eric asked as he took her plate and passed it to the head of the table where Grant was carving the turkey.

"About three months. I moved in during the first week of September."

"Which would you like, Mrs. Whitcomb, white or dark meat?" The question came from Grant. Mara noted the return to formality and answered in the same cool tone.

"White, please."

"And how do you like living in the country?" Eric continued. He was a very pleasant man with dark brown hair, vivid blue eyes, and a strong, open face. Mara could easily see why Vicky was so besotted with hm.

She smiled and accepted the plate he returned to her. "Actually, I like it very much. It's so peaceful and quiet here. I can put on my telephone answering machine and enjoy a whole day of uninterrupted painting whenever I like.''

"Would you like some cranberry sauce, Mara?" Alice asked, offering her the small cut-crystal dish.

"Thank you." Mara took a spoonful of the sauce and passed it to Eric.

Alice handed her the bowl of yams and as she did so, touched Mara's arm. "I can't tell you how pleased I am that you could spend Thanksgiving with us, my dear."

Mara smiled. "I'm enjoying it immensely. I've never had a Thanksgiving like this before." Seeing Alice's startled look, she shrugged. "It never seemed worth the effort to go to all this trouble for just two people. David and I usually just went to a restaurant for our traditional turkey and dressing."

What she had said was true, only her feelings were much more complex than that. There was a warm sense of belonging among these people, bonds of long-cemented friendships and familial feelings that aroused twinges of envy in her. Although she'd never consciously thought of it before, Mara realized now that she'd missed a great deal by not being part of a family unit. The closest she had come had been her marriage to David, but even that had not been the same. They had been a couple, but not a family. As Mara toyed with her food she wondered if she'd been wise to come. Her solitary life seemed so stark in comparison.

"Why, that's terrible!" Alice declared. "No one should be alone on holidays. It's a time for friends and families."

"Since Mara doesn't have a family I think we should invite her to spend Christmas with us also," Vicky inserted.

Alice looked at her daughter and smiled fondly. "That's a very good idea, darling. In fact, I insist upon it."

"I imagine Mrs. Whitcomb will be spending Christmas with Chuck Ainsley." Grant's cutting voice broke into the conversation before Mara could either accept or refuse the invitation. He picked up his wineglass and pinned her with a cold, challenging look over the rim. "In fact, I'm amazed she isn't with him now."

Mara met his glittering stare unflinchingly. She had been about to refuse the invitation, but now she'd be *damned* if she would. "Actually, that would be a little awkward, Mr. Sloane," she said, matching his cold formality. "Since Chuck and Helen are at this moment in the Bahamas on their honeymoon."

Grant's wineglass halted in midair, his features freezing as he stared back at her.

A delighted squeal erupted from Vicky. "Chuck and Helen are married! That's wonderful! When did this happen?"

"I attended the wedding yesterday, as a matter of fact." Mara smiled as her gaze switched to Vicky. "Since neither of them could take any time off for several months, they decided to use the long holiday weekend for a brief honeymoon."

There was a loud thump from the head of the table.

"Oh, darling! Look what you've done!" Janice cried, and began to dab at the spreading stain with her napkin. "You set your glass down so hard you spilled your wine. What on earth is the matter with you?"

Grant ignored her. A muscle twitched in his jaw as his steely gaze impaled Mara to the back of her chair. "This marriage? It hasn't upset you?" he questioned tautly.

"Upset me? Why should it upset me? Helen and Chuck are my best friends. I'm delighted."

"I was under the impression that you and Ainsley were more than just friends."

It was a statement, but Mara knew that Grant was really

asking a question, one to which he fully intended having an answer. She squirmed, uncomfortably aware that she had suddenly become the center of attention at the table. Damn Grant anyway! Mara picked up her knife and fork and calmly cut into the thick slice of turkey on her plate. "I don't know how you got that impression, Mr. Sloane." With a forkful of meat poised halfway to her mouth, she paused and slanted him a cool, dismissive look. "We've discussed your vivid imagination before, as I recall."

For a second he looked as if he wanted to choke her on the spot. A strange, intense emotion flared in his gray eyes, and Mara's spine tingled with alarm.

"Mara, dear, would you like to try this gelatin salad?" Alice inserted into the tense silence, attempting to divert the conversation. "It's a very old recipe that has been in our family for years."

Ignoring Grant, Mara accepted the dish with a grateful smile and spooned the quivering salad onto her plate. She wasn't going to allow him to spoil her enjoyment of the day. She couldn't understand why he was so angry, anyway.

After a few minutes, when it became obvious that the discussion was over, conversation around the table returned to normal. Mara tucked into the food on her plate with gusto, doing full justice to the excellent holiday fare. She kept her voice low, confining her conversation to her immediate table companions and ignoring the stony-faced man at the other end.

After dinner they all retired to the family room to watch the Thanksgiving Day football games on television. It was a large, informal room, paneled in a light, glossy oak. Massive beams spanned the cathedral ceiling, and a huge stone fireplace occupied one corner. On either side were enormous floor-to-ceiling bookcases. The wall-to-wall carpet was a deep slate blue. Twin sofas, in a slate blue,

gray, and copper print, sat at right angles, facing the
television and fireplace. Scattered about the room were
several comfortable chairs, upholstered in gray or copper.

Clinging possessively to Grant's arm, Janice managed
to steer him to one of the sofas. There was an empty
cushion beside him, but Mara ignored it and joined Vicky
and Eric on the matching sofa. Alice and the elder
Holmans occupied three armchairs.

Next to her, Vicky and Eric were talking in low
whispers, and Mara wondered just how long Grant
thought he could keep them apart. Eric was obviously
attracted to Vicky, but it was difficult to tell if his
emotional involvement matched hers. But when Mara
thought about it, she realized that wasn't really so surprising. Eric was a mature man. It was unlikely he'd wear his
emotions on his sleeve.

She tried to concentrate her attention on the television
screen but was uncomfortably aware of Grant's glowering
presence directly across from her. He didn't even pretend
to watch the game. Every time Mara looked up, his hard
gaze sliced right through her. His anger hadn't lessened
one iota, and she simply couldn't understand it.

When Alice announced that she was going to make
coffee Mara immediately volunteered to help—anything
to get out of that room. A few minutes later, as they left
the kitchen pushing the laden cart down the long central
hall toward the den, Mara placed a hand on Alice's arm.

"Alice, if you don't mind, I think I'll be on my way."
She glanced toward the long frosted-glass windows flank-
ing the front door. "It's getting late and if I don't start
soon it will be dark before I get home."

"Oh, my dear. Why don't you just stay and let one of us
drive you home later?"

"No, I couldn't do that," Mara refused quickly. She
simply couldn't endure another minute of Grant's hostility. "Anyway, I enjoy the walk through the woods."

"Well, I do wish you would stay a little longer, but if you insist upon walking, I suppose you should start now," Alice agreed reluctantly and pulled Mara's coat from the closet.

"I enjoyed the dinner very much, Alice. Thank you for inviting me." Mara darted a quick glance toward the den. "Would you mind saying good-bye to the others for me? I don't want to interrupt their game."

A touch of pink invaded Mara's cheeks as she caught Alice's sardonic look. The older woman obviously didn't buy her flimsy excuse, but she merely smiled and said, "Very well, Mara. I'll tell them."

"What's going on here?" Mara was just slipping her arms into her coat when Grant's voice cracked over them.

She jumped, then lifted her chin when she saw the challenging light in his eyes. "I'm leaving. Thank you very much for allowing me to share your Thanksgiving, Mr. Sloane," she stated stiffly. "I enjoyed it very much."

"I'll drive you home."

"No!" Mara returned instantly, but Grant had already stalked across the hall and was taking his sheepskin coat from the closet. "No . . . uh . . . look, this really isn't necessary," she stammered as she watched him shrug into the heavy coat. "As I told your mother, I really do prefer to walk."

Her own coat was still unbuttoned, and Grant's cool gaze raked over her, from the high neckline of her elegantly simple green wool dress, down over her nylon-clad legs, to the delicate brown suede pumps. "You're not dressed for walking through the woods," he stated emphatically and continued to button up his coat.

Mara bristled. "I walked over here dressed like this!"

"Well, you're not walking home. So stop arguing!"

Alice was watching them with barely concealed amusement, her interested gaze bouncing back and forth as though she were a spectator at a tennis match. Now she was laughing openly.

"Mara, I think you'd better do as Grant says. It's obvious that things are about to come to a head between you two, and I'm sure you'd prefer to have some privacy when that happens." At Mara's startled look Alice laughed even harder. She looked at her son and shook her head. "For heaven's sake, take the girl home and get this thing settled. I've put up with your bad humor for months now. I don't think I can take anymore."

"Neither can I," Grant bit out, stalking toward the door and dragging Mara along behind him.

She tried to hold back and dig in her heels, but it was like trying to stop a locomotive with her bare hands. Seeking support, she cast a desperate glance over her shoulder, and her heart sank. It was plain that Alice would be no help at all. She was already pushing the cart through the den door, smiling complacently.

Stumbling to keep up with Grant's long, ground-eating stride, Mara tried to pry his fingers loose from her arm. "Will you please let go of . . . ouch! That hurts!" she yelped when he tightened his grip.

He ignored her. Without a word, he marched out the door and down the front steps to the car parked in the drive. "What do you think you're doing?" Mara cried furiously, as she was bundled into the passenger seat. Grant merely slammed the door and walked around to the driver's side.

Before Mara could find the button to unlock the door he was climbing in behind the wheel. She turned to face him, her expression a mixture of bewilderment and anger. "What *is* the matter with you? And what do you think your girl friend is going to say when she realizes you've left with me?"

Grant's jaw was rigid. "Janice isn't my girl friend. Our

families have always been close and I've taken her out a few times, but we're just friends. Nothing more.''

"Well, someone had better tell her that, because I promise you, that isn't how she sees the relationship.''

"That's her problem. Janice and her pipe dreams have nothing to do with us. Now just shut up and sit still. We'll talk when we get to your place.''

Mara threw him a sharp look. Us? There was no *us!* What in the world was he talking about? She didn't understand any of this. Her mouth tight with irritation, Mara huddled close to the door and remained quiet for the rest of the journey.

When they reached her house she turned and opened her mouth to speak, but Grant was already climbing out of the car. She frowned as she watched him cross to her side. Oh, please do come in, Mr. Sloane, she thought sourly.

Inside, she barely had time to shrug out of her coat and toss it on a chair before Grant clamped his hands on her shoulders and spun her around. His strong-boned face was stiff with fury, his nostrils flared and white.

"Now, I want to know why you didn't tell me that Ainsley and Miss Thorn were engaged!''

Mara's emerald green eyes went wide with amazement. Why was he getting so worked up over Helen and Chuck's marriage? None of it made any sense! "It simply never occurred to me to tell you,'' she admitted truthfully.

"*It never occurred to you!*'' The steellike grip of his hands threatened to crush the delicate bones in her upper arms. "What the hell do you mean, it never occurred to you?'' A growing suspicion drew his brows together. "How long have you known that they planned to marry?'' he demanded.

Confusion marked Mara's expression, her eyes slightly out of focus as she struggled to remember. "I don't know. About three weeks, I guess.''

"So, you thought you'd let me suffer for a while, is that it? You knew I was going through hell, and you were enjoying every minute of it. Was this to be my punishment for misjudging you? Well, was it?" he shouted when she continued to stare at him, her eyes huge and uncomprehending. He gave her a hard shake that sent her hair bouncing around her shoulders like leaping tongues of fire. "Answer me, damn you!"

Mara struggled to break free. "Will you let go of me! I don't have any idea what you're raving about!"

Her words seemed to snap whatever control Grant had left. He hauled her up against his hard body, his arms encircling her like steel bands. "This is what I'm talking about," he grated as his head swooped.

He kissed her hungrily, desperately, like a man who has denied himself far too long, his mouth moving on hers as though he would devour her, absorb her into his body. The driving, possessive demand of the kiss forced her lips apart, and Grant gave a thick moan of satisfaction as his thrusting tongue began its intimate exploration.

At first Mara was too stunned to resist, her mind thrown into a state of utter confusion. Never had she envisioned anything like this between Grant and herself. His sudden, sensual assault had caught her completely off guard. But very quickly, shock gave way to awareness, and awareness to pure, unadulterated panic. The slightly musky male scent of him was all around her. The imprint of his hard body on her soft, yielding flesh set off a jangle of alarm bells through her nervous system. Mara struggled to break free of the devastating sensual embrace, but her hands were trapped between their bodies and the arms holding her would not budge. She moaned deep in her throat.

The small, desperate sound seemed to inflame Grant. His arms tightened around her body, lifting her toward him. He widened his stance and pressed her intimately close, and Mara's heart took off on a snare-drum roll as she was made fully aware of his desire for her. The kiss deepened hotly. Suddenly she could feel the heavy, muffled thud of his heart against her breasts. His large, powerful hands traveled up and down her back and hips, caressing and stroking as he molded her ever closer.

Mara was terrified. His unrestrained, passionate love-making had ignited her own suppressed desires. Their hot, searing flames licked through her veins like a wind-driven brush fire, threatening to destroy everything in its path, including her will to resist. Her body began to tremble. She didn't want to feel like this! Especially not with this man!

Grant shuddered violently and tore his mouth away from hers. "Oh, Mara, Mara. God, how I want you," he muttered thickly, burying his face in the side of her neck. The tip of his tongue traced erotic little patterns over her silken skin, as his mouth nibbled gently. "I've wanted you since the first moment I saw you. I've been going slowly out of my mind, imagining Ainsley kissing you, holding you, making love to you"—one hand moved up over her ribcage and cupped her breast—"touching you like this."

Mara sucked in a deep breath and closed her eyes. Oh, God! She had to stop this! The stroking touch of his fingers was driving her mad. Clenching her hands into small, tight fists, she pushed against his chest.

"Relax, honey," Grant breathed against her skin. His teeth tugged gently at her lobe, then his warm, moist breath trailed back over the delicate curve of her neck. Mara turned her head away and hunched her shoulder against his questing lips.

"No, Grant! Stop! This is crazy," she gasped.

He pulled back just far enough to look down into her face. There was a disturbed rhythm to his breathing, a burning, passionate look in his light gray eyes. "There's nothing crazy about it,'' he said forcefully. "I want you. And you want me. I admit I misjudged you. Very badly. Though that wasn't altogether my fault, since you deliberately misled me. But none of that is important. Not now.'' His hands came up to frame her face, the calloused fingers moving in a rough caress over her silken skin. "I want to make love to you,'' he whispered huskily. "I want to explore every inch of that beautiful body. I want to hear you cry out my name when I possess you.''

"No!'' Mara was shaken by the blatant way he stated his desire, the frankly sensual way he was looking at her. She wasn't cut out for affairs, no matter how much her body cried out for fulfillment. She simply was not emotionally equipped to handle that sort of thing. She was too vulnerable, too easily hurt. The circumstances of her life had caused her to retreat behind a wall of reserve. Emotional entanglements beyond the bonds of friendship had always been difficult for her. It had taken David months to break through her instinctive, self-protective barriers, and even then, only the strength of his love and his total commitment had allowed her to open her heart. She found the thought of a close, intimate relationship based on nothing more than physical desire repugnant. She shook her head slowly, her eyes wide with dismay. "No. I can't. I . . . I . . . just don't feel that way about you.''

For a moment Grant neither moved nor spoke. Then, frowning, he let his hands fall to his sides and watched as she took several cautious steps backwards. His eyes were narrowed dangerously, their icy glitter stabbing into her. In the heavy, thick silence, Mara could hear her heart pounding.

"I don't believe you,'' he said flatly. "Do you think I've forgotten the way you responded to me that night? If that damned phone hadn't interrupted us we would've made love then. And you know it.''

Mara's face flamed. She hated to be reminded of that night and the wanton, mindless way she had behaved. Swallowing hard, she backed away another step.

"I . . . it was the medication . . . the injection the doctor gave me," she stammered quickly. "I . . . wasn't myself."

Hot, fierce anger leaped in Grant's eyes. His face hardened, muscles clenching and unclenching beneath the tanned skin as he battled with his growing fury. He looked like a seething volcano about to erupt. Very slowly, he began to stalk toward her, and alarm feathered over Mara's skin, causing the short hairs on the back of her neck to stand on end.

"I still don't believe you. You want me as much as I want you. I've seen the way you look at me. Every time we're together you stare at me as though you can't get enough. Do you think I'm blind?"

"Oh, but you don't understand!" Mara was horrified at the construction he had put on her artistic perusal. She waved her hand in a weak, placating gesture. "If I was staring it was only because, as an artist, I think you're a fascinating male specimen."

"What! A *what!*" Grant was almost incoherent with rage, a dark, angry color suffusing his face. "That's how you see me? A male specimen? Just some *thing* to use as a subject for one of your damned paintings?"

Mara groaned inwardly. It had been entirely the wrong thing to say. She should have remembered the fragility of the male ego. "Well, I *am* an artist," she said weakly, in a feeble attempt to make him understand.

As he continued to advance toward her Mara backed away slowly, keeping a wary eye on him, until suddenly her back struck the high bar dividing the kitchen and living room. At that precise moment, Grant closed the gap between them. Leaning forward, he braced an arm on the counter on either side of her, trapping her.

He brought his face to within inches of hers. "From the moment you opened your door, that very first day, I wanted you," he snarled bitterly.

"No! I don't believe you!" Mara shook her head in insistent denial. "You were rude and nasty. You treated me as though—"

"Of course I did," he interrupted harshly. "I went there expecting to buy off a grasping, heartless little bitch like Enid Price. Instead I found myself confronted with the most ravishing creature I'd ever seen. It was all I could do to keep my hands off you. I was furious with myself for wanting you, and furious with you for being so damned desirable. I kept remembering what a fool my father had made of himself over Enid, how he had ruined his life and nearly killed my mother. I didn't want that to happen to me, yet just looking at you set me on fire."

Unnerved by his admission, Mara continued to shake her head mutely. She couldn't, she *wouldn't* believe any of this! Grant's eyes narrowed as he read the stubborn refusal in her face. This close she could see each individual black lash, and the way they curved away from his lids, the tiny specks of charcoal in the silvery irises. She shivered. He was so rawly male.

"I left there in a rage because I was sure Ainsley was your lover. When I got into my car I sat there and shook for fifteen minutes before I could calm down enough to drive." A raw resentment roughened his voice. "And every time I've seen you since, my desire for you has grown." He gave a short, mirthless laugh, one corner of his mouth quirking up in self-mockery. "I tried to hide it, but I was sure you knew how I felt."

With a sense of shock, Mara recalled the numerous times she had seen that shuttered look come over his face. She had wondered about it a few times but realized now that she hadn't been sufficiently interested to probe for its cause. How odd. That wasn't like her. Her artistic training had taught her to study people carefully, to probe beneath the surface, to seek out clues to their character and discover what drove them. It came so naturally to her it was almost a reflex action. Yet with Grant she had deliberately looked no deeper than the surface. She frowned, upset by the discovery, but was given no chance to examine her actions. Grant's low, furious voice cut into her thoughts like a sharp knife.

"And all the time I was behaving like a love-sick fool you didn't even see me," he snarled in icy resentment. Mara pressed back against the counter, straining to escape the barely contained rage that flared in his eyes. "But not anymore," he declared softly, menacingly. Smiling, he leaned closer.

A traitorous weakness caused Mara's knees to tremble as she felt the rippling muscles in the powerful thighs pressed against her own. The sensitive tips of her breasts tingled as they brushed against the hard wall of his chest. Her gaze locked with his and she had the oddest sensation of being drawn into the cool gray depths of his eyes. Pressing even harder against the counter, Mara sought escape from the magnetic pull on her senses. "Leave me alone," she pleaded in a breathless whisper.

Grant shook his head slowly. "Not on your life. I won't be ignored, and I won't be pushed away." His eyes narrowed on her face. A ruthless determination stamped the arrogantly male features. "I'm going to have you, Mara."

The blunt statement caused her heart to somersault right up into her throat. "No! You don't understand! I don't want to get involved. Not with you or anyone." Her voice had risen to a shrill pitch, in direct proportion to the panic that streaked through her veins.

"Tough," he declared callously, and with slow deliberation, bent his head and caught her mouth.

It was a soft, ardent kiss that made her heart thud

painfully against her ribcage. His firm male lips moved over hers in a mobile, sensual exploration, the tip of his tongue delicately tracing their curving outline before slipping between the fragile barrier in darting, teasing little forays meant to tantalize, not to satisfy. Mara quivered in helpless response.

A gleam of satisfaction glittered in Grant's eyes when he withdrew. "From now on, when you look at me you're going to see me. You're going to be aware of me with every cell in your body." His warm breath caressed her skin as he whispered the slightly threatening words, and Mara's eyes opened wide with alarm. Grant caught the betraying reaction and smiled. "I'm going to crawl right inside your skin, lady. I'm going to become as necessary to you as breathing. Before I'm through, you're going to beg me to make love to you." His voice was low and intimate, the silky tones adding a chilling degree of menace to the incredible statement.

Mara felt her stomach muscles twist into a sickening knot of fear. She shivered, her face a pale oval against the fiery brilliance of her hair, her green eyes wide and incredulous. She couldn't believe this was happening!

Grant straightened abruptly and stepped back. He stared down at her, his eyes deadly cold. Mara felt their touch like a physical blow. "I won't settle for anything less," he added after a moment.

He turned and walked out.

Mara leaned weakly against the bar, staring after him, her eyes blank with shock.

Chapter Nine

He didn't mean it. Of course he didn't mean it! He was angry, and his pride was hurt. That's all. When he calms down he'll forget all about those crazy, rash threats. It was a weak rationalization of Grant's astounding behavior, yet Mara clung to it tenaciously, repeating it over and over to herself, as if doing so would make it true.

But within a few days she was forced to admit that she had only been kidding herself. Grant had meant every word.

Quite suddenly he dominated her life. She saw him every day. If she stayed at home and painted, he came by. If she left the house, she bumped into him. It was a mystery to her how he managed it, but he seemed to know her every move. Everywhere she went, he was there: at the grocery store, the post office, the service station. Although he was careful never to say or do anything to which she could object, his attitude toward her very deliberately gave the impression that they were much more than just neighbors. He made it clear that he was staking his claim. All the signs were there for everyone to see: the smoldering gleam in his eyes; the husky, intimate tone of his voice; the possessive touch of his hand on her arm. If he had made love to her in public he couldn't have been more obvious.

And the local ladies seemed to find it all terribly romantic and titillating. Whenever Grant put on his besotted lover act they fairly swooned, sighing and fluttering their lashes in vicarious ecstasy. Mara wanted to scream.

But she didn't. Mara realized very quickly that she had two choices. She could lose her temper, which would probably only amuse him, or she could ignore him and hope he would finally tire of the game.

She chose to ignore him. She said nothing and did nothing to indicate that she was even aware of his ploy. His heavy-lidded, passionate gaze was met with a cool, bland look. Her voice remained carefully neutral when she was forced to speak to him. She was always polite, always self-possessed, her face a quiet, pleasant mask.

But if she fooled their interested observers, which she doubted, not for one minute did Mara think she had fooled Grant. There was amused mockery in his eyes every time she gave him a frosty look. He knew perfectly well he was getting under her skin.

At first she had been merely irritated. Then, as she realized his intent, her anger began to build. He wanted her, and he wanted everyone to know it. Daily his attentions became more marked, his pursuit more ardent. Mara was a very private, reserved person. Grant knew full well she would find such a public display embarrassing.

But what really irritated her, what sent her temper soaring from simmer to full boil, was the fact that he had made good his threat. He had forced his way into her life and she could no longer ignore him. By sheer hardheaded persistence he had made her aware of him, whether she wanted to be or not. He had so conditioned her to his presence that she found herself looking for him the minute she stepped from her car. When her phone rang, her first thought was, It's Grant. It made Mara furious to realize just how often her mind was occupied with thoughts of Grant. But the more her anger grew, the more she thought of him. It had become impossible to force his image from her mind.

Mara was sure their supposed romance was the main topic of conversation amoung the local gossips. Alice's unexpected visit a few weeks after Thanksgiving seemed to confirm her suspicions. It was the first time Alice had ever visited her in her home. And she had come alone, a circumstance Mara thought significant.

"How have you been, my dear?" Alice asked, following her into the small kitchen.

Mara filled two mugs with coffee and added a spoonful of sugar to Alice's. "Oh, I'm fine. I've been working like a beaver lately though."

"Yes. So Vicky has told me." Alice cocked her head to one side as she accepted the mug of coffee, her expression a mixture of amusement and curiosity. "Since you've been too busy to visit us, I thought I'd just come and see for myself if you were faring all right."

It was a gentle rebuke, but a rebuke all the same, and Mara flushed guiltily. Using the excuse of pressing work, she had not gone anywhere near Grant's home since Thankgsgiving. It wasn't exactly the truth. She *did* have enough work to keep her busy for years, but she was very self-disciplined and knew how to pace herself. There was no real need to rush.

Mara looked up and met the knowing gleam in Alice's gray eyes, then quickly looked away, her flush deepening. "I'm fine, as you can see."

"Yes," Alice agreed, smiling dryly.

She wandered back into the living room, cradling the steaming mug of coffee in her hands. "From what I hear, you and Grant seem to have made up your little quarrel." The comment was tossed over her shoulder as she idly inspected the room.

Mara stiffened. "No, not really."

Alice swung to face her. Her direct gaze was shrewd and slightly amused. "Being difficult, is he?"

"You could say that, yes."

"I thought as much. I was quite sure your relationship couldn't have progressed to the point everyone seems to think. You wouldn't be avoiding the ranch if it had."

Mara studied the swirling wisp of steam rising from her mug. "I'm sorry, Alice. I have no wish to avoid you and Vicky. It's just that . . ."

"It's just that my son won't take no for an answer. Right?"

Looking up, Mara gave her a wan smile and shrugged. "Something like that."

"Mmmmm. I see. Well, I feel I should warn you, my dear. Grant is a very determined man. He usually gets exactly what he wants."

"Not this time, he doesn't," Mara stated firmly.

Alice's expression grew thoughtful as she studied the defiant glitter in Mara's emerald green eyes. "Still, it seems a pity . . ." she mused softly, then her voice trailed away and she turned and continued her aimless tour of the room.

"You have a lovely place here, Mara. It gives the impression of space without being too large."

"Thank you. It's very comfortable, and it fits my needs perfectly." Mara smiled, grateful for the change of subject.

Alice finally came to a stop in front of the bookcase,

where her eyes fell on the small silver-framed picture. She picked it up and studied it. "This must be your husband."

"Yes, that's David."

"Do you still think of him often?" Alice asked, and Mara gasped, her eyes widening in surprise and shock.

She realized suddenly that she hadn't thought of David in weeks. In the long years since his death he had been with her constantly, a beloved, shadowy figure walking through her mind. Whether willingly or unwillingly, her heart had clung to his memory, while her body had merely gone through the motions of living. But somehow, in the last few weeks, she had let him go, and in doing so, had set herself free.

Dazed by the discovery, Mara looked at Alice and smiled wanly. "No, not as much as I once did. David will always be a part of me, a loving memory I'll always cherish, but I think I've finally accepted that the life we had together is over."

Alice continued to stare at the photo. "What was he like?" she asked, probing gently.

"As you can see, he was a ruggedly masculine man, very strong, very clever, determinedly aggressive. Rather like Grant," Mara said without thinking, and then froze as the words hit her. Why had she never thought of that before?

Her knees gave way beneath her and she sat down on the sofa with a thump. She could barely breathe for the tumultuous emotions that clogged her chest. Those words had just come tumbling out of nowhere, but as soon as they were said she recognized them as absolute truth. For months she had turned a blind eye to Grant, refusing to see him as a man. He had existed in her mind on a purely impersonal, one-dimensional level. He was a neighbor, an acquaintance—no more. But quite obviously he had registered on her subconscious, and in a way that both startled

and frightened her. Had she sensed intuitively that he
possessed those very same traits she had found so wildly
attractive in David? Had she retreated from the knowledge
by simply burying it in her subconscious?

"Well, I must say, that was a very revealing statement," Alice commented sagely. She sat down next to
Mara on the sofa. "And I see from the shocked expression
on your face that you think so too."

Mara looked at her with bewildered green eyes.
"I . . . I . . . it simply never occurred to me before."

"Mmmm. Well, the description you just gave certainly
fits my son." She studied Mara. "Tell me something.
How would your David react if he were in Grant's shoes
right now?"

"*Oh my God!*" The words came rushing out in a
horrified, breathless whisper. Every last vestige of color
drained from Mara's shocked face as her imagination
painted a vivid picture in her mind. She knew with
certainty that David would do exactly what Grant was
doing. During their courtship he had used gentle persistence to overcome her reservations, but she knew that, had
he met any real opposition, he would have simply forced
his way into her life. Men like David and Grant did not
accept defeat. Whatever they did, they played to win.

Mara shivered as she recalled how single-minded David
had been when fighting a case in court. He had been clever
and determined, aggressive to the point of ruthlessness
when making a point. Many times she had seen him back
an obstructive witness into a corner with the sheer force of
his personality and extract exactly the testimony he had
been seeking.

Grant's recent pursuit of her had been just as forceful,
just as determined.

Mara came out of her daze to find Alice watching her.
She lifted her hands to cover her pale cheeks. "Well," she

said, laughing shakily. "It seems I'm cursed with stubborn men in my life."

"Or blessed," Alice returned softly. She gave Mara a
long, intent look, then smiled and patted her hand. "Don't
worry about it. It will all work out. You'll see." Abruptly
her manner became brisk and she placed her empty mug
on the coffee table.

"I really must be going now, dear. I only came by to
see how you were and to make sure you were still coming
to our Christmas party this Saturday."

"Of course I'm coming. I'm looking forward to it,"
Mara lied.

When Alice had gone Mara tried to paint, but after only
a few hours she was forced to give it up as a lost cause.
For once she could not concentrate on her work. Much to
her disgust, her mind kept returning to Grant and the
discovery she had made.

Could she possibly be attracted to him? She had often
heard that people were drawn, over and over, to the same
type. Lord, she hoped not! The thought was so disturbing
that all she could do was pace back and forth across the
floor. To become involved with Grant would be commit-
ting emotional suicide. She had only just recovered from
the pain of loving David. She wouldn't be able to survive
something like that a second time.

The thought of falling in love again terrified Mara. Not
that love was what Grant was offering. He wanted her. He
had stated that quite plainly. But Mara was not the type of
woman who went in for affairs. She simply could not
handle them. When she gave of herself she gave everything. Grant, like most men, could probably indulge in a
brief affair and walk away unscathed when it ended. Mara
couldn't. In any intimate relationship her emotions would
always be involved. When the affair was over she would
be broken into a million little pieces.

Mara knew how emotionally devastating it was to lose someone you loved. But at least when she had lost David she'd had the comfort of knowing that theirs had been a mutual commitment, a love so strong only death could have ended it. But to be used, to be drained of all the love you had to give and then be tossed aside . . . The words trailed away in her mind, her body shuddering in sick reaction at the thought.

Mara walked slowly to the glass wall at the end of the studio and stared at the gaunt beauty of the forest. A gusting "Texas blue norther" had stripped the trees of their brilliant foliage. Intertwined skeletal branches stood out in sharp relief against the deepening blue of the evening sky. Mara crossed her arms over her midriff, rubbing her elbows in agitation. She felt raw, vulnerable, as exposed as the denuded forest.

The next morning Mara awoke feeling wooden-headed. The bout of self-examination had resulted, inevitably, in a throbbing head, but this time she had not let it get out of hand. At the first sign of distress she had taken her medication and climbed into bed. The sun had barely set when she closed her eyes and drifted off into a deep, pain-dissolving sleep.

Sluggishly, Mara turned her head to cast a bleary-eyed look at the bedside clock and groaned. With a sigh, she threw back the covers and dragged herself out of bed.

After a hot shower, Mara emerged feeling slightly less frayed around the edges and dressed in her oldest, softest pair of jeans and a blue chambray work shirt. Since she was in no shape to paint, she decided to spend what was left of the morning sorting through the pile of sketches that had accumulated during the past few months.

A vigorous brushing sent her long hair shimmering down her back like a sheet of fire. A light application of moisturizing lotion and a few strokes with a soft copper lip gloss completed her morning grooming. After making the bed, Mara stepped into a pair of soft leather moccasins and padded toward the kitchen.

She was pouring her second cup of coffee when someone knocked on the door. Mara stared at it, frowning. Was it Grant? Yesterday, for the first time, he hadn't appeared at all, and she had been very conscious of his absence, a fact that had made her furious with both Grant and herself.

She walked slowly toward the door, her doeskin-clad feet making no sound on the hardwood floor. Her first inclination was to simply ignore the knock, but after a brief hesitation common sense won out and she reached for the knob. After all, it might not be Grant. She opened the door a few inches and peeped cautiously around the edge.

"Good morning, Mara. I hope I haven't called at an inconvenient time." Eric Delany stood outside, his coat collar turned up against the gusting north wind.

"Eric! How nice to see you." Mara stepped back and opened the door wide. "Come in before you freeze to death."

"Thanks." He stepped inside, rubbing his hands together briskly. The cold freshness of the outdoors radiated from him. "I hope you don't mind me dropping by this way, Mara. I know you're busy, but if you could spare a few minutes I'd like to talk to you."

"Of course." She hung his coat on the brass rack by the door and motioned toward the furniture grouping in front of the fireplace. "Why don't you have a seat while I get us some coffee?"

"Thanks. That sounds great."

"What did you want to see me about?" she asked from over the counter as she prepared the small coffee tray.

Eric turned sideways on the sofa to face her. "I came to see if it was at all possible to get my name on your waiting list. Ever since I became a partner in my father's construction company he's been nagging me to have a portrait painted." He grinned ruefully, as though the idea didn't appeal to him at all.

Mara set the tray down on the coffee table and handed him his cup. Tucking one foot under her, she curled up in the corner of the couch and cradled her steaming mug between her hands. "I'm afraid I don't do formal portraits, Eric. The type of work I do wouldn't be at all suited to an executive office."

"Which is precisely why I want you to do it," he replied firmly. "If I must have my portrait painted I at least want to look human, not like some stiff-necked, pompous ass."

Mara laughed. She knew exactly what he meant. She had seen hundreds of those rigid, haughty portraits lining boardroom walls and plush executive suites. She abhorred them. Nothing could induce her to paint that type of portrait.

"I can understand how you feel, Eric, but I think before you make up your mind, you'd better see an example of my work." She placed her mug on the tray and stood up. "Come up to my studio and have a look at the one I'm working on now."

In the loft, Eric stopped dead still when Mara led him to the easel that held Vicky's portrait. He stared at it for a long time, neither moving nor speaking. Mara could see that he was caught in the grip of some powerful emotion. He was completely spellbound, unable to tear his eyes away from Vicky's wistful beauty. If Mara had had any doubts about his feelings, they were gone now.

She had painted Vicky as she'd found her that day in the woods—sitting on a rock, her chin propped on her drawn-up knees. Her eyes were soft with longing as she gazed into the distance at something just out of reach. You could see the unfulfilled desire etched in the lovely, innocent features, feel the quiet desperation in the tautly held body. It was a poignant, ethereal painting—infinitely sad. And quite, quite beautiful.

Eric swallowed hard, his eyes still glued to Vicky's face. "I don't suppose you'd allow me to buy this painting?" he asked quietly.

Mara sighed and shook her head. "I'm sorry, Eric. Grant commissioned this portrait. I can't sell it to anyone else."

"Of course. I should have realized that." Turning his head, he gave her an apologetic smile; then his eyes were immediately drawn back to the canvas.

The strong face bore a look of hungry yearning that tugged at Mara's heartstrings in a way she could not ignore. "Eric, I can't sell you the painting, but I can let you have a few of the preliminary sketches, if you'd like."

"I'd love to have them," he assured her instantly, and without a word, Mara went to her portfolio and fished out the sketches, then spread them out on the worktable.

"There you are. Take your pick. Or take the whole lot, if you want them."

"Are you kidding? Of course I want them." He laughed excitedly, his gaze jumping from one sketch to another. "I'll gladly pay whatever you're asking."

"Don't be silly," Mara retorted. "I'm not going to charge you for these. Take them. They're yours." When he began to protest Mara simply gathered them up, stuck them into a manila folder, and handed it to him. "Here, take them."

Eric looked stunned. "Mara . . . I don't know how to thank you . . ."

"Then don't," she said quickly. "Just take them and enjoy them." She slipped her arm through his and drew him toward the stairs. "Now come on. Let's have another cup of coffee."

They had just settled themselves on the sofa when someone knocked on the door. Mara looked up, her mouth firming. This time she was sure it was Grant. There was no mistaking that peremptory knock.

"Excuse me a moment, Eric." Scowling, Mara stalked to the door and jerked it open.

"Hello, Mara." Grant smiled mockingly as he stepped inside and pulled the door from her hand, shutting it behind him. He knew perfectly well she had not intended to invite him in. His narrowed gaze went beyond her to the man sitting on the sofa, then swung immediately back to her face. He stared at her intently for a moment. Then, without warning, he bent and placed a soft kiss on her parted lips. Straightening, he smiled directly into her wide, startled eyes, his own glinting with amusement as his fingertips trailed caressingly over her cheek.

Mara gasped and took a jerky step backward, but before she could protest, Grant turned and sauntered into the living room.

"Hello, Eric." He took off his coat and tossed it over the back of a chair. "I thought that was your car outside. What brings you here?" he asked casually, bending over to check the coffee tray.

Eric looked back and forth between Grant and Mara and grinned. He hadn't missed that bit of intimate byplay near the door. "I came to see if I could commission Mara to do a portrait of me," he replied.

Grant walked over to the bar and took another mug from the rack, then returned to the living room and helped himself to the coffee. Lowering his huge frame into one of the comfortable wing-backed chairs, he stretched his long legs out in front of him and settled back.

Mara stared at him in open-mouthed consternation as he made himself at home. *Anyone would think he lived here!*

"I see," Grant said quietly. He sipped the hot brew, eyeing his friend over the rim of the coffee mug. "And did

Mara agree?'' The softly worded question held a note of challenge, as though he didn't altogether approve of the arrangement.

Mara stepped forward. ''Yes, I did,'' she stated defiantly. Who the devil did he think he was, using that tone? She gave him a withering look. Resuming her seat on the couch, she picked up the coffee pot. ''Would you like another cup, Eric?''

''No, thank you, Mara. I really must be going.'' He placed his mug on the table and stood up. When Mara started to follow he stopped her. ''No, don't get up. I can see myself out.''

''I'll come with you,'' Grant said, rolling to his feet. ''I'd like to have a word with you.''

Eric looked amused. ''Sure. Why not?''

At the door Grant turned and gave Mara a hard look. ''I'll be right back.''

When he returned a few minutes later she was in the kitchen washing the coffee mugs. She slanted him an annoyed look as he strolled over and perched on one of the barstools on the other side of the counter, but she set her mouth in a firm line and stubbornly refused to say a word.

Grant leaned forward and propped his chin in his hand. ''It won't work, you know,'' he said enigmatically.

''What are you talking about?'' Mara eyed him warily, her gaze sharpening as she noted his self-satisfied expression. The talk with Eric must have pleased him. He was positively smug.

''You're not going to use Eric as a shield against me. It won't work.''

Mara swished a mug through the rinse water and slammed it down on the draining rack. ''Don't be ridiculous! The thought never entered my head. And anyway, Eric is in love with Vicky.''

''I know. That's why I've just given him my permission to date my sister.''

Mara's head jerked up, her face alive with pleasure. "Oh, Grant. That's marvelous! Vicky will be over the moon." A warm smile softened her features. "What made you change your mind?"

"You."

"Me?" She gaped at him, completely bewildered, her face blank with surprise. "How could I make you change your mind?"

The hard, well-shaped mouth quirked slightly. "It occurred to me that when a man is denied the woman of his choice, he might seek consolation elsewhere." Grant's gray eyes locked possessively on her face. "If Eric is dating my sister, at least I'll know he's not hanging around you."

"What!" Mara's shocked expression gave way to a ferocious glare. "I don't believe this! Do you mean to say you're willing to sacrifice your own sister, just so you can . . . can . . ."

"Make love to you," Grant supplied softly, laughing as Mara's face flamed. "Yes. Though I'd hardly call it a sacrifice, since Vicky's crazy about him. Eric's a good man. He'll take care of her. My only objection to the match is the difference in their ages, but time will solve that problem."

Mara dried her hands on the towel and flung it onto the counter. Planting her fists on her hips, she glared at him, her eyes shooting green flames. "Why? Why are you doing this? You can't be that desperate for a woman. Even your mother told me you have a very active sex life," she goaded nastily, hoping to make him so angry he'd give up in disgust.

But Grant merely smiled. "I'm not desperate for just any woman," he explained patiently. "I want you."

"Well, you can't have me!" she flared.

Mara was breathing hard, struggling to hold on to her temper. What on earth had happened to the composed, self-contained woman she'd been just a few weeks ago? Grant had happened, that's what, she told herself grimly. She had held him at bay with a force field of indifference, but now he had crashed his way through that invisible protective barrier and forced her to see him, really see him, as a man. He kept her stirred up and off balance, her emotions in such a constant turmoil that she barely recognized herself.

Why? Why was he going to this much trouble? Mara frowned as she studied his ruggedly handsome face. It couldn't be just sex. There was an aura of raw power about him, a vital masculinity that was unmistakable. He could probably have his choice of a dozen women. So why was he pursuing her so relentlessly? Was it revenge, because she had hurt his pride? Or was it . . . ? Her face froze as an idea occurred to her, her eyes narrowing into two bits of glittering green ice.

"Is this just another attempt to drive me away?" she demanded suspiciously. "Did you think if you pestered me enough, if you made a big enough nuisance of yourself, I'd finally give up and move back to Houston?"

Grant raised his eyebrows. *"Could* I force you to move?"

"When donkeys fly!" she blazed inelegantly, strangely angered by his failure to deny her accusation.

"Good," he replied with irritating satisfaction. "Because if you did I'd just come after you and haul you back. I'm not about to let you get away from me now."

"Ohhh," Mara stormed in exasperation. "I give up."

She stalked around the end of the counter, intent only on getting away from him, and headed toward the door to her bedroom. As she came level with him, Grant swiveled the barstool around, reached out, and snared her wrist. With one quick jerk, he pulled her against his hard body, trapping her between his outstretched legs.

"I've been waiting to hear you say that," he teased.

"Will . . . you . . . let . . . me . . . go!" Mara said in a rage, straining against his hold.

Grant laughed and locked his hands behind her back. "Never," he said succinctly. "Haven't you realized that yet?" He was smiling down into her face, but his eyes were completely serious. Mara's heart squeezed painfully.

Since the night he had declared his intention to have her, his manner toward her had altered dramatically. Now, instead of becoming angry when she tried to discourage him, he treated her with an amused indulgence that Mara found maddening. He was relaxed and confident, almost smug, as though he knew he would eventually win. Grant in action was a study in hardheaded patience and determination. She had tried everything she could think of—cold indifference, sarcasm, anger, even downright rudeness—but nothing seemed to faze him. He just kept coming, like a tidal wave.

She leaned back against his encircling arms and put as much distance between them as possible, eyeing him warily. "Grant," she began on a warning note, "I've told you repeatedly that I'm not going to become involved with you." Her voice rose to a shrill pitch, her composure slipping as she saw the deviltry dancing in his gray eyes. "Why won't you *listen*?"

Grant laughed and cocked his head to one side. "Did you miss me yesterday?" he asked teasingly.

Oh, yes. She had missed him, all right. That was the problem. Very cleverly, Grant had become an integral part of her life, so that now, when he wasn't there she was uneasy, unable to concentrate. Against her will, he was becoming important to her. But for nothing in the world would she let him know how aware of him she had become.

Mara raised her delicately arched brows. "Why?" she asked with feigned innocence. "Were you gone?"

A rumble of laughter vibrated deep in Grant's chest. "Oh, lady. You're going to regret all those little barbs one of these days," he purred warningly, drawing her inexorably nearer.

A shiver of anticipation slithered up Mara's spine. Her heart began to thump painfully. Despite common sense, despite all the bracing lectures she had given herself, she could not ignore the powerful attraction that flared between them. It was basic, elemental, and her body reacted to it instinctively, though her mind continued to resist.

Her hands came up between them, pushing ineffectively against his chest. "Grant, stop. You mustn't—"

In the next second his mouth covered hers. Mara's strangled cry was swallowed by his engulfing kiss. He quelled her frantic struggles easily, folding her in his arms and pulling her close, trapping her with his masculine strength. His mouth moved hotly, demandingly against hers, as his caressing hands molded her to his aroused body. Mara's skin tingled with awareness as she felt his hard male need pressed against her soft flesh. The relentless pressure of his mouth forced her lips apart. The rigid tip of his tongue flicked against her teeth, stirring an unwanted curl of excitement in her, but she stubbornly refused to give in to it.

"Open your mouth to me, honey. Let me taste you."

The seductive whisper sent a quiver of longing through Mara, and she shook her head, fighting desperately to resist the urgent pull on her senses. "No!"

The word had barely left her lips when his tongue thrust into the sweet, moist warmth of her mouth. A shaft of intense pleasure shot through Mara and reason deserted her. With a soft, fatalistic moan, she melted against him. Without conscious thought her hands crept upward to encircle his neck and pull him closer. At once his arms tightened. He kissed her deeply. hungrily, sending a hot wave of desire surging through her.

His mouth released hers slowly to trail a warm, moist path across her cheek. Mara shivered in delight as his lips, his teasing tongue, gently stroked the delicate swirls of her ear.

"Grant, you must stop," she breathed weakly. "We can't . . . Oh, Grant . . . "

His hand had deftly unbuttoned her shirt and slipped inside to cup her aching breast.

"Yes, we can. We can do whatever we want." She caught her breath as his thumb circled the hardened tip of her breast. "And right now I want to make love to you. And you want me to."

His tongue darted into her ear and a delicate shudder rippled through Mara. "Don't you?" His warm breath caressed her skin as his mouth moved back to hover over hers. "You want me to hold you, to kiss you." He caught her lower lip and sucked gently. "Don't you?" he insisted in a soft, relentless voice. His tongue teased the corner of her mouth, and Mara made an inarticulate little sound.

"Tell me, babe. Say it." The words were breathed against her parted lips, then his tongue slipped inside and gently touched the tip of hers, and withdrew.

Mara groaned and pressed closer. "Yes, oh yes," she cried in a small, desperate voice.

A low growl of satisfaction rumbled in his chest as his lips crushed hers. Mara strained aginst him, kissing him back with frantic need.

The pressure of his thighs held her close while his hands gently stroked and kneaded her breasts. The rough caress of his calloused fingers on her satin-smooth skin was oddly pleasing, sending delightful little shivers chasing up her spine. Mara groaned and slid her fingers into his hair. Her sensitive fingertips explored the shape of his head and held him close as his lips left hers to begin a slow, leisurely trek downward.

Neither of them heard the quick rap on the door just before Vicky pushed it open and stepped inside.

"Mara, I . . . Oops!"

Shock washed over Mara. She jerked free of Grant's embrace, her face flaming a deep crimson as she caught sight of Vicky's stunned expression.

The girl was rooted to a spot just inside the door, her hand over her mouth, her eyes huge with surprise and amusement. "I'm sorry . . . I didn't mean . . . I had no idea . . . I mean . . . Heavens!" The incoherent babble came to a halt as words failed her.

"Don't worry about it, Vicky," Grant drawled smoothly. "Your timing leaves a lot to be desired, but we'll forgive you." If he was at all embarrassed he certainly didn't show it. Very casually, as though he did it every day of the week, he reached over and began to button up Mara's gaping shirt.

That jolted her out of her trance instantly. With a harsh cry, she slapped his hands away and whirled around. She closed her eyes in agonized embarrassment as her trembling fingers moved awkwardly over the task. Grant's soft laughter made her blood boil, and she shot him a killing glance over her shoulder. Damn him! she fumed silently.

Her anger didn't touch him. Slipping his arm firmly around her waist, Grant pulled her with him as he started toward the door. "Come on. See me out. And stop glowering at me like that," he said, chuckling.

Mara had been knocked so completely off balance that she was trembling all over. She moved jerkily beside him, her mind racing. How in heaven am I going to explain that torrid little scene to Vicky? she thought frantically. She couldn't even claim that he had been kissing her against her will. She had been participating fully, reveling in the sensations he had aroused, loving the feel of his hard body, the taste of his skin, the wonderful, clean male scent of him. A shudder quaked through Mara and she closed her eyes. *Good Lord! I must be losing my mind.*

At the door Grant turned and gripped her shoulders. Laughter was still brimming in his eyes. "I'll pick you up for the party tomorrow night at eight."

"No, I—"

He bent and silenced her with a quick, hard kiss. "I'll pick you up."

The implacable tone left no room for argument. Mara clamped her lips together and glared at him in impotent wrath.

Grinning, Grant gave her cheek a playful tap, turned on his heel, and left.

As the door closed behind him Mara turned her reluctant gaze on Vicky, wincing inwardly when she saw the avid curiosity sparkling in her eyes.

Vicky opened her mouth to speak, but Mara silenced her with a quickly snapped, "I don't want to talk about it, Vicky."

Chapter Ten

Mara gave her hair one last flick with the comb and stepped back to survey the results in the mirror. Shining red hair framed the delicate oval face and cascaded around her shoulder like a fiery cloud. A light application of makeup gave her creamy skin a luminescent quality, and a touch of silver blue eyeshadow enhanced the beauty of her eyes. A soft rose lip gloss glistened on her lips.

Her jerseylike silk dress was a shimmering midnight blue, elegantly simple, with a deep V-neckline and a straight, clinging skirt, slit to the knee on one side. The full, flowing, tightly cuffed chiffon sleeves somehow made the gown appear both modest and alluring. A delicate pearl and diamond pendant nestled just above the shadowy cleft of her breasts, its finely wrought gold chain barely visible against her skin. Matching earrings winked through the loose cloud of red hair.

Mara stared at her reflection, feeling strangely nervous and keyed up. For some reason she felt as though she were standing on the edge of a precipice.

A knock on the door made her jump. After one last, hasty inspection, Mara picked up her mink jacket and small gold evening bag and headed for the front door. With her hand on the knob, she paused, squared her shoulders, and schooled her features into a cool mask. When she jerked the door open her eyes widened and the mask slipped a bit at the sheer overpowering look of the man standing there. In a black evening suit and a white silk shirt, Grant was devastating.

Swallowing hard, Mara moved back and allowed him to enter, then closed the door quietly and turned to face him. She watched his eyes widen and blaze hotly as they slid over her hair and face and then moved down over the figure-hugging gown. When he lifted his eyes to hers, Mara's lungs suddenly ceased to function. The smoldering look, the taut expression, were so blatantly sensual they made her toes curl.

"God, you're beautiful." His voice was low and urgent, desire throbbing in the deep tones. His compelling gaze locked with hers. "I want you, Mara. Very much. And I'm going to have you."

A lightning shaft of excitement zigzagged through Mara at the calmly worded statement. Shaken, she stared at her own reflection in the silvery gray eyes, and her heart began to pound. With sudden, stunning clarity, the truth she had been avoiding for weeks, possibly even months, overtook her. She was in love with him. Subconsciously, from the very beginning, she had known that this powerful, overwhelming, intense man was a danger to her well-organized existence, and she had thrust the knowledge out of sight. But now it would not be denied. Mara drew a painful breath into her tight chest and stepped back, color draining from her face.

"What is it? What's the matter?" Grant's brows met as he noted her pallor and the wide, dazed eyes. He reached out a hand as if to comfort her, but Mara quickly spun away.

Four jerky steps put a safe distance between them. She didn't think she could bear to have him touch her. Not now. She was too shaken, too vulnerable.

"Nothing! Nothing's wrong," she answered quickly. "I . . . I just thought of something I forgot to do. That's all." Taking a deep breath, she fixed a false smile on her face. "I'm ready if you are."

A pulse beat wildly in her throat as his probing gaze searched her face. For a moment she thought he was going to challenge her flimsy excuse, but then, without a word, he stepped forward and took her mink jacket from her nerveless fingers. Quivering with relief, Mara turned and slipped her arms into the sleeves.

The party was in full swing when they reached Grant's home. The minute they stepped over the threshold they were swept up in a tide of laughter and animated conversation. Both the living room and the wide entrance hall, which ran the depth of the house, were filled with people, all of whom seemed to be talking at once, their voices merging into an indistinguishable hum. The soft strains of a popular tune floating from the stereo provided a pleasing background to the muted din.

Mara felt her nerves tighten as they entered the crowded living room. She had never been much of a party person, even under normal circumstances. In her present emotional state the last thing she wanted was to spend the evening with a crowd of strangers, pretending to enjoy herself. But she would. She had to, somehow.

On the short drive from her home Mara had lectured herself severely. Her feelings for Grant were crazy, impossible. She had to conquer them, root them out of her system, before they grew too deep, their hold too strong. It shouldn't be too difficult. Love, in order to grow, had to be nourished and cared for, tended carefully. And that was something she had no intention of doing.

After greeting his mother, Grant took Mara around the room. His arm remained firmly around her waist as he led her from one group of people to another. In each case he introduced her as their new neighbor, but the look in his eyes and the husky pitch of his voice when he spoke her name implied that there was much more to their relationship than that. The determined way he kept Mara beside him drew several speculative looks. With a sinking feeling in the pit of her stomach, Mara knew the gossips were going to have a field day.

They had almost made a circle of the room when a uniformed waiter paused to offer them a glass of champagne from the silver tray he was carrying. Grant took one but Mara demurred.

"Does alcohol make you ill, or do you object to it strictly on moral principles?" he inquired, slanting her a teasing look as the man turned away.

"Neither," she muttered uncomfortably, trying to focus her gaze on anything but the wicked look in those pale gray eyes. "I simply don't care for the taste. Or the aftereffects."

"Ah, but in small doses alcohol can be very beneficial. It helps you to unwind and relax." He pulled her closer and bent his head to whisper, "It even makes some people more passionate, more . . . uninhibited."

"Since I have no intention of shedding my inhibitions, I'll pass, thanks," Mara retorted.

The laughter glinting in Grant's eyes immediately faded. "Ah, but you will shed them, sweetheart, when the time comes," he murmured. "Your response to my lovemaking has left little doubt of that."

Mara stared at him wordlessly. Hot, embarrassed color flooded her cheeks, and just as quickly drained away.

"Don't. Please don't," she begged in a shaken whisper, tearing her gaze away from the compelling male features.

Oh, God, she was a fool to love this man. The knowledge that he merely wanted her physically tore at her heart. But what hurt even more was the undeniable fact that she wanted him also. She loved him. And because she loved him, she desired him. Her emotional and physical needs were inseparable.

"All right. We won't talk about it now," Grant agreed resignedly. "But I'm warning you, Mara. I won't be put off much longer. You can't pretend to be indifferent to me. Not anymore." The arm at her waist tightened and urged her forward. "Now come on. Let's dance. And for heaven's sake, smile."

When they reached the area where several couples were swaying together to the soft music, he stopped and turned her into his arms. A basic instinct for self-preservation made Mara resist when he pulled her close, and the action earned her a taunting smile. Holding her wary gaze, Grant very firmly curved both of her hands around his neck. Slowly, sensuously, he let his own hands slide down the chiffon-covered arms to her shoulders, then down the elegant curve of her spine, molding her to him.

Mara felt herself go weak. The imprint of his body, the seductive pressure of his thighs brushing against hers as they swayed to the dreamy music, turned her knees to jelly and robbed her of the will to resist. It was heaven to be held in his arms.

Through the thin silk of her dress Mara felt his hands moving slowly over her back and hips, his fingertips tracing her spine in an erotic caress. Desire, fierce and hot, quaked through Mara's body, and she trembled.

Laughing softly, triumphantly, Grant bent to nuzzle the tender skin just behind her ear, burying his face in the mass of silky hair. "Now tell me you don't think of me that way, that you don't want me.'' His teeth tugged gently at her lobe, and Mara closed her eyes in mute surrender. There was nothing she could say to that.

The party took on an unreal quality for Mara. Still reeling from the shock of her newly discovered love and the searing desire Grant had aroused in her, she was barely conscious of the crowd of people, of the constant hum of voices, the clink of glasses, the steady, rhythmic beat of the music that wove its way through the cheerful babble. She danced and laughed and somehow managed to exchange small talk with a number of people but was scarcely aware of doing so. She was too conscious of the large, virile man hovering possessively at her side.

Late in the evening, as she was dancing with a rather talkative young man, Mara cast a bored look over his shoulder and instantly her heart contracted. Hot, searing jealousy stabbed through her as she watched Janice Holman and Grant moving slowly around the floor to the soft, romantic music.

The blond girl was stroking the back of his neck, gazing adoringly up at him, her red-lacquered nails combing sensuously through the luxuriant hair just above his collar. Grant didn't seem to mind. He was smiling down into Janice's glowing face as though he found her enchanting.

Biting her lip, Mara quickly looked away. Well, what had she expected? Grant had never mentioned love. He made no secret of wanting her, but then he probably wanted Janice too. That thought sat on her heart like wet cement.

What did it matter, anyway, she told herself dismally. Even if he did love her it wouldn't change anything. She couldn't go through that agony again. She simply couldn't. Love was too risky, too painful.

Her unhappiness deepened with every passing minute. Mara walked through the rest of the evening overwhelmed by the sickening jealousy that gnawed at her. It was an emotion she had never before experienced. The only other man Mara had ever loved had been David, and he had returned her love wholeheartedly. She had never had any reason to doubt him or to know this agony.

It was sheer misery, trying to pretend that nothing was wrong, pasting a false smile on her face and letting the laughter and party talk wash over her. Through it all Grant kept her close to his side, an arm draped casually over her shoulders. Mara found his closeness almost unbearable. Her feelings were so raw that she couldn't bring herself to meet his eyes. She was terrified that all she was feeling— the love, the tearing jealousy, the utter despair—would be clearly visible in her eyes. She couldn't give Grant that kind of weapon.

Finally Mara could stand it no longer; she had to get away. Tomorrow, when she had her emotions under control, she would deal with Grant. But not now. Not tonight. If she let Grant take her home, if she were alone with him, she was bound to give herself away.

Driven by sheer panic, while Grant was dancing with one of his mother's friends, Mara slipped out the door, down the hall, and into the room where the women's wraps had been stored. A quick search produced her mink jacket and she slipped her arms into the sleeves as she headed for the door. In the act of reaching for the knob, she paused, then recrossed the room and stepped out through the French doors onto the patio.

The north wind knifed through her. It plastered her thin silk gown to her legs, and against her nylon-clad skin it felt like a sheet of ice. Mara burrowed deeper into the short jacket and kept her head down against the buffeting wind, following the brick path around to the front of the house. Briefly, she considered taking the shortcut through the woods but dismissed the idea as impractical. The narrow trail was barely discernible in the daytime. At night it would be invisible. Mara didn't look forward to the three-mile walk along the road, but she really had little choice. Gritting her teeth against the biting cold, she started down the drive.

It soon became painfully obvious that high-heeled evening sandals were never intended as walking gear. By the time she reached the road she had turned her ankle twice. And to make matters worse, her feet felt like two blocks of ice.

She had barely made it around the first curve in the road when the beam of a car's headlights sliced through the darkness. Panic clawed at her. Mara's heart bounced around like a Ping-Pong ball, and she began to look for a place to hide. But it was too late. Brakes squealed, and the silver Continental slid to a stop beside her.

The passenger door was thrust open. "Get in," Grant snapped.

Mara hesitated for just a second, biting her lip as she took in his thunderous expression; then, without a word, she meekly obeyed. She had no doubt that he would pick her up and put her in the car if she refused.

The instant she had settled into the seat the powerful engine roared to life, sending up a spray of dirt and gravel from beneath the spinning wheels. Mara shuddered violently as the warm air from the heater flowed around her.

The atmosphere in the car was tense, the silence heavy and threatening. Very cautiously, she peered at Grant out of the corner of her eye. Her throat tightened when she encountered his set profile.

Mara cleared her throat. "Grant . . . I'm . . ."

"Save it," he commanded. "We'll talk at your place."

Tires squealed in protest when he swung the car off the highway onto her narrow drive. Mara was forced to grip the edge of her seat to keep from being slammed against the door. She opened her mouth to protest, then thought better of it. His anger beat against her like pounding waves.

By the time they entered her living room, Mara's stomach was twisted in a hard knot. There was no way to avoid this final confrontation; it had been building between them for weeks. But oh, how she dreaded it, especially now, loving him as she did. With a calm she was far from feeling, Mara removed her coat and tossed it over the back of a chair. Then, taking a firm hold on her courage, she turned to face him.

Her eyes grew wide as Grant stormed past her and tossed his overcoat onto the same chair. They grew even wider when his suit jacket followed. Swinging around to face her, his eyes burning hotly, he jerked the tie from his neck and added it to the growing pile of clothing. His gaze never left her as, very slowly, he began to unbutton his shirt.

Mara swallowed hard. Good Lord! How much undressing did he intend to do? When he began to pull his shirt from the waistband of his trousers she took an instinctive step backwards. "Wh—what are you doing?"

The gold links were removed from his cuffs and dropped into his pocket. Grant shrugged out of his silk shirt and tossed it onto the heap of discarded clothing. "I'm going to tear down that wall you've built around yourself, once and for all," he informed her calmly. "There'll be no more denying what you feel. No more running." His eyes locked with hers and Mara saw the harsh determination, the unyielding possessiveness burning in the gray depths. It wasn't a bluff.

She paled. Shaking her head, she began to back away. "Grant, this is crazy," she protested feebly, staring at him with wide, disbelieving eyes. Despite the tumultuous emotions that tore at her, Mara couldn't pull her gaze away from his broad, muscular chest. She had never seen him without his shirt before, and he was absolutely magnificent. Everything about the man was overwhelmingly masculine—the breadth of his shoulders, the sinewy muscles that bunched and rippled beneath the tanned skin, the mat of dark curling hair that covered his chest, then narrowed as it reached his taut, flat abdomen. Blood roared in Mara's ears and her mouth went suddenly dry.

When he started toward her she shook her head and held her hands up as though to ward him off. "Grant, please. You . . . you said we'd talk."

Holding her panic-stricken gaze, Grant shook his head slowly. "And no more talking." Each word was rapped out clearly, precisely, the hard finality in his tone causing her heart to turn over.

Bowing to the inevitable, Mara stopped and stood rooted to the spot. Fear and undeniable excitement sparkled in her eyes as Grant covered the distance between them in two giant strides. He grasped her shoulders and pulled her against him with a force that drove the air from her lungs.

"I've been one big ache since the day we met. But no more," he breathed huskily. Then his head began its slow descent.

Mara braced herself for his angry assault, but it never came.

Gently, tenderly, his mouth claimed hers, and a piercing sweetness stabbed at her heart. The soft, mobile kiss was the most exquisitely sensual thing she had ever experienced, the pleasure so intense, so complete, she thought she would die of it. Trembling with joy and wonder, Mara felt Grant's hands slide down her back, his arms wrap around her and gather her close. The kiss went on endlessly, a soft, persuasive seduction that stirred her senses and left her wanting more.

Then, very slowly, Grant pulled his mouth from hers to look down into her face. Incapable of speech or movement, Mara remained as she was—head thrown back, eyes closed, breathing deeply through parted lips. Her expression was one of rapture, her features blurred with passion.

"Look at me, Mara," he whispered unevenly.

Slowly, as though in a trance, her lashes fluttered upward, and Grant drew in a sharp, hissing breath at what he saw in her eyes. It was all there, everything she was feeling, and seeing it, his own eyes flared hotly. Then his face hardened.

"Do you want me, Mara?" he probed insistently.

"Yes . . . no . . . oh, I don't . . ."

The driving force of his kiss silenced her, making dust of her pathetic resistance. The small fires ignited by his first kiss now burst into flames. And the flames quickly built into an inferno as his mouth grew more demanding.

Mara's hands slid upward over the warm, hard-muscled chest, her fingers tangling briefly in the mat of springy hair that covered it before gliding over his bare shoulders.

His mouth left hers and moved slowly across her cheek to her ear. "Mara. Oh, God, I want you." His voice was raw with desire.

Turning her face into the side of his neck, Mara breathed deeply. "Grant," she whispered, struggling to break through the heady cloud. "We can't—"

"Yes we *can*," he said fiercely. "And we're going to. Right now." Swiftly, he lifted her into his arms and carried her into the bedroom. Next to the bed he stood her on her feet and turned her back into his arms, his lips finding hers with a savage hunger. Helpless against the sensual onslaught, Mara returned the kiss, barely aware of him easing down her zipper or of the silky blue dress slithering to the floor. Sanity returned ever so briefly when his hands pushed her narrow slip straps from her shoulders. She tore her mouth away from his.

"No, Grant." Mara couldn't breathe properly, and the protest came out as a barely audible gasp. A violent shudder quaked through her as his tongue traced a line of fire down the side of her neck. She opened her mouth to protest again, but then the slip slid silently to the floor and his hands were roaming over her skin. Desire flooded through her, hot and swift, making reason and thought impossible.

She stood docilely, trembling with need as he slowly removed her few remaining items of clothing. For just a moment his eyes devoured her; then he scooped her up in his arms and placed her gently on the bed. His own clothing was removed with considerably more haste, and within seconds he was beside her.

"Oh, God! I've waited so long for this." The words were choked out just before his mouth closed over hers. Her hands cupped his head to hold him close and they strained against one another in wild, desperate need.

In some remote part of her brain Mara knew that she was going to regret this, that she would pay dearly for this brief moment of happiness. But that was later, and this was now, and she loved and needed him so.

His mouth trailed across her cheek to her ear and his tongue traced the delicate swirls. Traveling downward over her neck and shoulders, his lips nibbled and tasted. As he gently nuzzled the soft, sloping curves of her breasts Mara sighed and threaded her fingers into his hair to urge him closer. His lips and tongue caressed the warm fullness with maddening leisure, slowly circling the rosy crests, but never touching them. Mara writhed with longing under the tantalizing exploration.

"Please, Grant. Please!" she gasped.

With a smile in his voice, he whispered, "Oh, yes, love," and a moan of ecstasy escaped Mara's throat as his lips closed over a hardened nipple.

As his lips and tongue caressed her breast, his hand stroked the length of her body, from throat to knee, then back again. Responding to the tactile exploration, Mara let her own hands roam free, her sensitive fingers threading through the mat of curling chest hair to stroke the masculine nipples, then glide downward over his ribcage to his taut, flat stomach.

The soft hiss of Grant's sharply indrawn breath halted her hand on its path of discovery.

"Oh, God! Don't stop now," he cried hoarsely. But Mara could not move. She was trembling, weak with longing.

Grant raised himself up on one elbow and looked down at her. His face was flushed and rigid with desire. Watching her closely, he slid his hand across her flat stomach and down over her leg to her knee. Then, very deliberately, his fingers stroked upward over the silkiness of her inner thigh. The intimate caress sent a searing heat rushing through Mara's body, and she moaned and closed her eyes. A smile of blatant satisfaction curved Grant's hard mouth.

He kissed her then, driving her to the edge of madness before he finally pulled back and whispered against her lips, "You're going to have to say it, sweetheart."

"Please, Grant."

"Please what? Tell me. What is it you want?"

Mara gazed at him with wide, vulnerable eyes, knowing that he was demanding his pound of flesh, and that she was powerless to deny him. "I want you," she whispered. "I need you. Oh, please, Grant. Love me. Please!"

He smiled again, warmly this time. Cupping her face in his hands, he stared deep into her eyes. "Oh, I intend to, darling. I intend to," he murmured softly, as he shifted his weight so that his body covered hers.

A heavy frost had come during the night. In the pearly, predawn light icy crystals lay over the brown stubble of grass like a misty bridal veil. Every tree branch, every twig, glistened with a thin coating of ice. Mara could feel the cold air seeping through the windowpane as she stood at the back door, gazing out at the incredibly beautiful scene. A brilliant cardinal left a trail of tiny tracks in the virgin whiteness as he hopped along the edge of the deck in search of the crumbs Mara threw out every morning. She watched him with brooding eyes. *What was she going to do?*

"So there you are," Grant said softly from behind her, and Mara stiffened instantly.

Grasping her coffee mug with both hands to stop their trembling, she closed her eyes and took a deep breath, then turned very slowly.

Grant stood with his hip braced against the kitchen counter, his arms folded over his bare chest, wearing only the dark trousers he had discarded so hastily the night before. Mara's heart thudded painfully. Her eyes drank in the virile beauty of his half-clad body, remembering the feel of it against her own. She gritted her teeth, fighting the warm weakness that flooded her.

"Good morning," she said with deceptive calm.

Grant cocked one brow and grinned crookedly. His gaze went beyond her to the window. "It's hardly that yet." The grin relaxed into a coaxing smile, and he held out his hand. "Come back to bed, sweetheart. I missed you."

Mara's heart jerked violently. The husky pitch of his voice, the tousled, sleepy-eyed look, the unmistakable invitation in his words, all dragged at her senses, but she fought determinedly against the magnetic pull. Ignoring his outstretched hand, she walked over to the sink. With studied calm she poured the remainder of her coffee down the drain, rinsed out her cup, and turned it upside down in the rack. Then, tightening the belt on her white velour robe, she turned and met his eyes.

"Grant . . . about last night." She paused and bit her lower lip, then hurried on. "It . . . it was a mistake. It should never have happened."

Grant pushed himself away from the counter. His smile gave way to wariness, shock and pain mingling in his eyes. "It wasn't a mistake, Mara," he stated quietly, firmly. "I love you. I want to marry you."

For an instant joy flared inside Mara, sparkling in her eyes and giving her face a radiant glow. But just as quickly the pain came crashing down on her. Deep down she had known all along that Grant cared for her, but she had refused to see it—had not wanted to see it. How much easier the whole thing would be if he didn't love her. Feeling sick, Mara looked at him and uttered the words she knew had to be said. "It makes no difference. I—I can't marry you."

"Why not?" Grant demanded sharply. "I love you. You love me. Where's the problem?"

Her head jerked up. "How do you know I love you?"

Grant raised one hand and cupped her chin. His eyes were warm with remembered pleasure as he smiled down into her face. "You told me so last night. Don't you remember?"

Had she? Then she remembered, and her face flooded with color. Last night, at the height of their lovemaking, just as they had reached the pinnacle of exquisite pleasure, she had cried out her love for him, unable to suppress it in that moment of supreme happiness and fulfillment. They had drifted down from the soaring heights of passion into a contented sleep, entwined in each other's arms, replete and sated, and she had forgotten the impassioned declaration. Until now.

Pulling free of Grant's hold, Mara walked back to the door and gazed out at the ice-coated clearing. "That admission slipped out in a moment of passion."

"Are you saying now that it isn't true?" His voice took on a hard edge as anger crept in.

Mara turned her head and looked at him over her shoulder. Torment darkened her eyes to a deep jade. The temptation to deny her feelings was strong, but she couldn't do it. After a moment of taut silence her shoulders slumped. "No, I'm not saying that," she replied dejectedly, her gaze returning to the wintery scene. "What I *am* saying is—it makes no difference."

Her heart feeling like a lead weight in her chest, Mara turned and faced him. "Love doesn't last, Grant. You know that as well as I. Look at your parents . . . and mine." She gave a short, mirthless laugh. "If it doesn't die a natural death, then fate steps in and snatches it away from you." Her voice was wobbling now and her throat was constricted painfully but, telling herself it had to be said, she lifted her chin and continued. "And when that happens you want to curl up and die. Well, I won't go through that again. I *can't* go through that again."

Her words hung in the thick silence that stretched between them. A spasm of pain flickered across Grant's face for just an instant; then, as she watched, his expression hardened and his jaw thrust out in that familiar, belligerently determined manner.

"Do you honestly think you can turn your back on what we have and feel nothing?" he demanded. "No pain, no regret?"

"No, of course not," Mara answered with an agitated gesture. "But don't you see? It's better to end it now while it's new, before it has a chance to grow."

"It's too late, Mara," he said flatly. "Your feelings may be new, but I've been in love with you for months. To lose you now would be pure hell." His eyes impaled her, refusing to let her look away. "Can you do that to someone you love, Mara? Can you deliberately inflict that kind of pain?"

Mara looked stricken as she stared back at him. With stunning accuracy, he had homed in on the one argument that would sway her. She could remember the agonizing grief she had suffered when David died, the complete

desolation. The very thought of willfully causing Grant
that kind of pain made her feel sick.

Until that moment she had never even considered the
situation except from her own point of view. Her grief
over David had been a lonely, solitary thing, involving no
one else, and somehow she had thought of this parting in
the same light. Now she knew that was not the case.
Could she do it? Could she hurt him like that? *No!* her
heart screamed. And yet . . . if she didn't . . .

Confusion and uncertainty flickered across her expres-
sive face as she struggled to find an answer. Seeing it,
Grant pressed his advantage.

"Mara, look at me," he commanded softly, and when
she did, her gaze was caught and held by the warm light of
love that burned in his eyes. He stepped forward, smiling
gently. "Sweetheart, I can't promise that someday, in the
far-distant future, I won't die before you. That's something none of us know. But I *can* promise that I will love
you, and only you, for all the days of my life."

His voice was low and urgent, and the ring of sincerity
in the deep tones pulled painfully at her heartstrings. Mara
wanted to run to him and throw her arms around his neck,
but her long-standing fear held her back. She stood rooted
to the floor, staring at him through unshed tears, twisting
her hands together convulsively.

When she made no move to come to him Grant walked
toward her slowly and, with great tenderness, pulled her
into his arms. "Please, sweetheart. Please say yes. I want
so much for you to be my wife. My lover. The mother of
my children." His breath stirred the hair at her temple as
he murmured urgently, "Marry me, darling. I don't think
I could live without you."

The tender, evocative words broke the last, slender
thread of resistance. Sliding her arms around his waist,
Mara closed her eyes and rested her head against his chest.
For a long time she stood perfectly still within the circle of

his arms, listening to the reassuring thud of his heart pounding beneath her ear. At last, fear conquered, her resolve firm, she lifted her head and looked directly into his eyes.

"I love you, Grant," she whispered. "I tried to ignore it. I tried to deny it. I even tried to run away from it. But I find that I can't." She gazed at him silently for a moment, her eyes swimming with emotion. Finally, taking a deep breath, she uttered the words he had been waiting to hear. "I'll marry you, darling. Whenever you say."

"Tomorrow," Grant said thickly as he sought her mouth.

Mara closed her eyes and gave herself up to the pure bliss that suddenly permeated her very soul. For so long she had thought that love and happiness would always elude her. She had pictured herself growing old alone, always an observer of life, never an active participant. Now that picture was fading, pushed out of her mind by the procession of images that danced across the back of her eyelids: Grant with a laughing child in each arm, evenings spent in quiet companionship, nights filled with passion and love, a life of sharing, needing, giving. The possibilities were limitless.

Four exciting
First Love from Silhouette
romances yours for 15 days—*free!*

These are the books that girls everywhere are reading and talking about, the most popular teen novels being published today. They're about things that matter most to young women, with stories that mirror their innermost thoughts and feelings, and characters so real they seem like friends.

To show you how special First Love from Silhouette is, we'd like to send you or your daughter four exciting books to look over for 15 days—absolutely free—as an introduction to the First Love from Silhouette Book Club.℠ If you enjoy them as much as we believe you will, keep them and pay the invoice enclosed with your trial shipment. Or return them at no charge.

As a member of the Club, you will get First Love from Silhouette books regularly—delivered right to your home. Four new books every month for only $1.95 each. You'll always be among the first to get them, and you'll never miss a title. There are never any delivery charges and you're under no obligation to buy anything at any time. Plus, as a special bonus, you'll receive a *free* subscription to the First Love from Silhouette Book Club newsletter!

So don't wait. To receive your four books, fill out and mail the coupon below *today!*

First Love from Silhouette is a service mark and registered trademark.
